St. Louis Community College

Forest Park
Florissant Valley
Meramec

Instructional Resources
St. Louis, Missouri

THE THREE-CORNERED
HAT

THE TRUE History of an Affair current in certain Tales and Ballads, here written down as & how it befell, by Don PEDRO ANTONIO DE ALARCÓN, Bachelor in Philosophy & Theology, &c. Now translated out of the Spanish by Martin Armstrong, with an Introduction by Gerald Brenan, & illustrated by Roger Duvoisin

THE THREE-CORNERED HAT

Don PEDRO ANTONIO DE ALARCÓN,

Amereon House

To the Reader

It is our pleasure to keep available uncommon titles and to this end, at the time of publication, we have used the best available sources. To aid catalogers and collectors, this title is printed in an edition limited to 150 copies. It has been manufactured in the United States to American Library Association standards on permanent, durable, acid-free paper. ————— **Enjoy!**

To order, contact
Amereon House,
the publishing division of
Amereon Ltd.
Post Office Box 1200
Mattituck, New York 11952-9500

Contents

INTRODUCTION :

AUTHOR'S PREFACE :

   I. Of when the thing happened   1
   II. Of how folk lived in those days   4
   III. *Do ut des*   6
   IV. A woman seen from without   10
   V. A man seen from without and within   15
   VI. The accomplishments of our couple   19
   VII. The foundations of felicity   22
   VIII. The man with the three-cornered Hat   24
   IX. Gee up, donkey!   30
   X. Heard in the arbor   32
   XI. The bombardment of Pampeluna   36
   XII. Tithes and firstfruits   45
   XIII. Said the jackdaw to the crow   50
   XIV. Weasel's advice   55
   XV. Prosaic farewell   62
   XVI. A bird of evil omen   69
   XVII. A rustic Mayor   72
   XVIII. In which it is seen that Miller Lucas was
      a very light sleeper   76

[CONTENTS]

XIX.	*Voces clamantes in deserto*	78
XX.	Suspicion and reality	81
XXI.	On guard, my lord!	92
XXII.	Weasel excels himself	100
XXIII.	Again the desert & the aforementioned voices	103
XXIV.	A monarch of that time	105
XXV.	Weasel's star	109
XXVI.	Reaction	112
XXVII.	In the King's name!	113
XXVIII.	Half-past twelve and a fine night!	118
XXIX.	*Post Nubila . . . Diana*	123
XXX.	A great Lady	124
XXXI.	The pains of retribution	126
XXXII.	Faith moves mountains	133
XXXIII.	Well? And what about you?	137
XXXIV.	Her Ladyship's a fine woman too!	143
XXXV.	Imperial decree	148
XXXVI.	Conclusion, Moral, & Epilogue	151

INTRODUCTION

THE ancient and honorable city of Guadix in which Pedro Antonio
de Alarcón was born is not much visited by tourists. It is a noisy,
dusty little place, lying a little to the east of Granada and containing
today some twenty thousand inhabitants, though in his time it had
far less. It has a late baroque cathedral of no particular interest, a few
ramshackle palaces of fairly recent date, and the usual Moorish cas-
tle. But it has also its Barrio de Santiago, where a third of the popu-
lation lives in caves, and this provides a good reason for visiting it.
For these caves, cut out of the soft red sandstone as cheese is cut with
a knife, are one of the most curious sights in Europe. They are in-
comparably more picturesque than the famous gipsies' caves of the
Sacro Monte at Granada because they are scattered along a cliff-face
that is cut up into such an intricate tangle of dry ravines that it re-

sembles a lunar landscape. One seeing them for the first time has the impression of being in Persia or Turkey.

To the people of Guadix, however, these caves are not a subject for civic pride, and Alarcón, though he was soaked in the romantic ideas of his time, never mentions them. To him and to his fellow citizens the greatness of the city lay in its history. A far more ancient place than either Granada or Seville, Guadix already had a thousand years or so of settled life behind it when the Romans took it from the Carthaginians and called it Acci. At that time it was a mining center as well as a rich agricultural market, and practised the cult of an Iberian moon goddess whom the Romans assimilated to Isis. At the end of the first century seven missionaries arrived from Rome to spread the doctrines of Christianity; their leader, San Torcuato, who may have been a disciple of St. Paul, became its first bishop. It is for this reason that the Bishop of Guadix takes precedence today over all other bishops in the country.

Six hundred years later the Arabs arrived and rebuilt the city a few miles away on its present site. Acci became Wad-Ash and under that name it flourished and produced famous poets and writers, all of a mystical tendency. Then in 1489 it surrendered, without a siege, to Ferdinand and Isabella and sank to being a small provincial town, its affairs managed by a clique of leading families who owned most of the land and who traced their descent from the original Christian settlers or *pobladores*. The division between rich and poor was great and has gone on increasing to the present day.

It was in this dull, self-centered little town, with its stiff formal society, dominated by the bishop and the cathedral canons and by a few rich families, that Alarcón was born on March 10, 1833. He came of an old family that had been ruined during the Napoleonic Wars and so his father could not afford to send him to Granada University. Instead he went to school with the Franciscans and then to the Seminary, where he studied theology. But as a lively, intelligent youth with a strong bent for literature he felt no vocation for the priesthood; in fact his only desire was to get away from Guadix. By writing for a literary magazine he was able to raise a little money; with this, in 1853, he went off without informing his parents to Cadiz and then to Granada. In the following year a revolution took place in Spain, led by two generals, O'Donnell and Espartero, with the object of forcing Queen Isabella to introduce a Liberal constitution. The whole of the South of Spain rose. Alarcón, who was just twenty-one, put himself at the head of the mob, seized an arms deposit, and stormed the Capitanía General. A new government was set up in Madrid and the young writer became a local celebrity.

The Romantic fever was still at its height. The poetry of Espronceda and the Duke of Rivas fed the young with fiery Byronic sentiments and with stirring recollections of the past greatness of Spain. Alarcón, who regarded himself as a poet, founded a literary club, La Cuerda Granadina, whose members wore the open collars and flowing black ties that denoted a dedication to the Muses; and, since Radicalism in politics usually went with Romanticism in literature, he brought out a daily journal that put forward the most extreme views. He was so successful in this that he was invited to become the editor of a Madrid paper, *El Látigo*, or *The Whip*, which was fiercely republican and anti-clerical.

But Alarcón was the child of a happy and religious home; his revolt was simply the reaction of a talented and romantic young man against the stifling atmosphere of the seminary where he had been educated. His heart was not really engaged in the career of a revolutionary and a priest-eater, and now an event occurred that made him suddenly realize this. An article he had written for his paper led to his being challenged to a duel by a Venezuelan poet, José García Quevedo. Alarcón fired and missed and his adversary then emptied his barrel in the air. This act of generosity made such an impression on the young editor that he resigned from his paper and retired to Segovia to live quietly and earn his living by literary journalism. At the same time there was a change in the political scene, for Espartero, the leader of the Progresista party, was forced out of office by a *coup d'état* and O'Donnell became the head of a government that called itself Liberal but was really Conservative. Radical opinions went out of fashion because they no longer held out any hope of leading to office.

Two years later, in 1859, General O'Donnell led an expedition to Africa which succeeded in capturing Tetuan. Alarcón was in an embittered mood, for a play he had written had been hissed off the stage, and he also wished to atone for the guilt he felt at having expressed such violent opinions and to recover the good opinion of the world. He therefore enlisted in the expeditionary force as a private soldier. Every night in Africa he wrote down his impressions, and when the war ended in a ferment of patriotic enthusiasm, he published this diary in book form as *Diario de un Testigo en la Guerra de Africa*.

Its success was immediate: fifty thousand copies were sold in a fortnight, and from this moment he never looked back. A succession of amorous adventures in the fashionable world of Madrid ended in 1865 in a very happy marriage which strengthened his religious feelings. He was elected three times in succession as deputy to the Congress for Guadix in support of O'Donnell's party, the Unión Liberal. From that he moved on by gradual stages to a minor diplomatic post and was eventually made a Councillor of State and a member of the Spanish Academy.

Meanwhile, in spite of the interruptions caused by his political career, Pedro de Alarcón was writing. The romantic attitudes of his youth had been slowly modified by experience. What he kept was a love of melodramatic situations and characters, but in his best books he contrived to make them convincing. The short stories and novellas on which his fame rests were written at rather long intervals between 1859 and 1881. In 1875 he brought out a long novel, *El Escándalo*, or *The Scandal*, a *roman à clef* which caused a great flutter. Another novel, *El Niño de la Bola*, followed in 1880 and then he stopped writing, just as the novels of that great master of realism,

Pérez Galdós, were beginning to make Alarcón's appear a little dated. When he died in 1891 he had shed most of his Liberal views and was regarded, a little unjustly, as a clerical and reactionary.

As I have said, it is for a few of his short stories and novellas that Alarcón is remembered today. They are most of them set some distance in the past, like Galdós' *Episodios Nacionales*, and designed to give a robust and racy view of Spanish life and character.

El Sombrero de Tres Picos, or *The Three-Cornered Hat*, which came out in 1874, is by a long way the best thing that Alarcón ever wrote. The story had obsessed him for many years. He first heard it, he tells us, in the form of a ballad recited by an old shepherd; and this ballad, or one very like it, is printed in Agustín Durán's great collection of ballads, the *Romancero General*, where it is called the *Ballad of the Miller of Arcos de la Frontera*. Durán had taken it from one of those *pliegos sueltos* or broadsheets which were sold in the street by blind men, usually after they had sung or recited them to a guitar accompaniment.

This bawdy tale, which no doubt had a long history before it was turned into a ballad, could not without a good deal of alteration be made the basis of a nineteenth-century novel. Alarcón had to preserve the chastity of the two wives while allowing their husbands to fear the worst, and this demanded a much more complicated plot. But being good at plots, he was able to contrive that the reader should be kept in suspense almost to the end. He laid the scene at Guadix, of whose countryside he gives a delightful picture, and drew the various characters with care and skill, making them just such as the plot required. The Corregidor—with his pride and stupidity and his terror of his formidable wife—is particularly successful; the conversations between him and his *alguacil* Garduña are in the best comic style. Behind scenes like these lies a deep and ironical understanding of how the municipal machinery in small Andalusian towns really worked.

The Three-Cornered Hat was an immediate success in Spain and an even greater success in foreign countries. Its *andalucismo* fitted in exactly with the foreigner's conception of Spanish life and character, whereas Galdós' far more mature and penetrating novels of Madrid life attracted little attention. For more than a century now the traveller from the North has come to Spain in search of the picturesque and has found in the wild scenery, in the bandits and the bull-fights and the dramatic attitudes, something that he lacked in his own tame and well-ordered country. And this was to some extent the case with Alarcón too. Under a thin covering of nineteenth-century romanticism he shared the very different romanticism of the baroque age with its harsh tones and its love of contrasts and melodrama. In this story he softened the outlines in the true Andalusian manner to make a delicious comedy.

The balanced and symmetrical form of *El Sombrero de Tres Picos* made it especially suitable as a subject for opera or ballet. In 1896 Hugo Wolf wrote an opera on it which he called *Der Corregidor* and in 1919 Diaghileff put it on the stage as a ballet, *The Three-Cornered Hat*, with music by Manuel de Falla and costumes and décor by Picasso. Léonide Massine, who had first prepared himself by a prolonged study of *flamenco* dancing with a Sevillian gipsy called Felix, took the part of the miller, Tamara Karsavina that of the miller's wife, and Leon Woizikovsky gave a deliciously grotesque interpretation of the Corregidor. The ballet was an immense success in the small circle of people who at that time appreciated Diaghileff's productions; it established once and for all Massine's reputation as a great dancer and choreographer. In 1934 it was revived by Colonel de Basil's company with Massine, Tamara Toumanova, and David Lichine taking the leading parts, and has since been given by the Ballet Theatre (as *Tricorne*), the Sadler's Wells company, the Ballet Russe de Monte Carlo, and in a condensed version by José Greco. Admirable as Alarcón's little novel is, it is this superb and subtle ballet that has given the *The Three-Cornered Hat* its world-wide reputation.

GERALD BRENAN

Author's Preface

FEW SPANIARDS, *even among those who have no scholarship or book-learning, can be ignorant of the popular story which serves as basis for the present little work.*

A rough goatherd, who had never wandered beyond the remote Farm on which he was born, was the first that we heard relate it. He was one of those country-folk, quite unlettered but with a natural wisdom and humor, who play so large a part in our national literature under the title of picaros. *Whenever there was any festivity at the Farm, a wedding or a christening, or the solemn visit of the landlord, it was his business to arrange the games and pantomimes, to act as clown and juggler and to recite tales and ballads; and it was on one of these occasions (now almost a lifetime since; that is to say, more than thirty-five years ago) that it was his task to enchant and dazzle our (comparative) innocence with the story in verse of* The Corregidor and the Miller's Wife, *or, if you like,* The Miller and the Corregidor's Wife, *which we offer to the public today under the more transcendental and philosophical title (for so does the gravity of these days require) of* The Three-Cornered Hat.

We remember, by the same token, that when the goatherd gave them such good measure, the marriageable girls there as-

sembled turned very red; from which their mothers concluded that the story was a little free. Whereupon they, in their turn, came near to turning the goatherd black and blue. But poor Repela (for such was the goatherd's name) did not mince matters and answered that there was no reason for any one to be so shocked, since there was nothing in his Tale that even nuns and children of four didn't know.

"If you don't believe it, just think a moment," he said. "What do we gather from the story of The Corregidor and the Miller's Wife? That married folk sleep together, and that no husband likes another man to sleep with his wife."

"And that's truth!" said the mothers, hearing the laughter of their daughters.

"The proof that Gaffer Repela is right," remarked the father of the bridegroom at this point, "is that all here present, great and small, know well enough that tonight, after the dance is over, Johnny and Manolilla are going to sleep for the first time in the fine marriage-bed which Aunt Gabriela has just shown to the girls so that they could admire the embroideries of the pillows."

"And, what's more," said the bride's grandfather, "in the book of Doctrine and even in Sermons, they speak to children of all these things of nature, so that they should understand the meaning of the long barrenness of our Lady Saint Anne, the chastity of Joseph, Judith's stratagem, and many other miracles that I don't remember at the moment. Consequently..."

"*It's all right, it's all right, Gaffer Repela!*" *exclaimed the girls, plucking up courage.* "*Tell us your Tale again: it's very interesting.*"

"*And very decent too,*" *continued the grandfather.* "*For there's nothing recommended in it that's bad; and it doesn't teach folk to be bad; and as for those that are, they get their deserts* ..."

"*Go on! Tell it again!*" *decreed the mothers.*

And Gaffer Repela set about reciting the ballad again; and, when all had considered it in the light of that honest criticism, they found there was nothing in it to take exception to; which is equivalent to saying that they granted the necessary licence.

In the course of years we have heard many different versions of that same adventure of The Miller and the Corregidor's Wife, *always from the lips of the Wag of the farm or village, after the order of the now dead Repela, and we have read it too in print in various* Blind Man's Ballads, *and finally in the famous* Romancero *of the unforgettable Don Agustín Durán.*

At bottom the subject is always identical; tragi-comical, waggish and terribly epigrammatic, like all the dramatic moral lessons of which our people are so fond; but the form, the accidental mechanism, the casual developments, are different, very different, from the way our goatherd told the tale, so different that he could never have told any of the aforementioned versions at the Farm, nor the printed ones either, unless all decent girls had stopped their ears; and if he had, he would certainly have had his eyes scratched out by their mothers. To such a point have the low-minded clowns of other provinces stretched and twisted the traditional matter which was so savorous, discreet, and comely in the version of the classic Repela.

It is a long time, then, since first we conceived the intention of reasserting the truth of the matter, restoring to the strange history in question its primitive character, which we have never doubted was that in which decency is triumphant. And how could we doubt it? That type of Tales, in passing from hand to hand of the common folk, is never denaturalized into something finer, more delicate and decent; what happens is that it is tarnished and mutilated at the touch of clumsiness and vulgarity.

Such is the history of the present book. And so let us put grist to the mill; I mean, let us make a beginning of the Tale of The Corregidor and the Miller's Wife, *not without the hope that your sane judgment (oh, respectable public!) "after you have read it and crossed yourselves more often than if you had seen the devil," as Estebanillo González said at the beginning of his, "will hold it worthy and deserving of publication."*

P. A. DE ALARCÓN

July 1874

I. OF WHEN
THE THING HAPPENED

IT WAS at the beginning of this long century which is already drawing to a close. The year is not precisely known; it is certain only that it was after 4 and before 8.

There still reigned at that time in Spain, Don Carlos IV, of Bourbon, *by the Grace of God* according to the coins, and by oversight or especial grace of Bonaparte according to the French bulletins. The other sovereigns of Europe descended from Louis XIV had already lost their crowns, and the chief of them his head, in the disastrous storm which swept this age-worn quarter of the world after 1789.

Nor was that the only singularity of our country in those times. The Soldier of the Revolution, son of an obscure Corsican lawyer, victor at Rivoli, the Pyramids, Marengo, and a hundred other battles, had just crowned himself with the crown of Charlemagne and completely transfigured the face of Europe, creating and suppressing nations, blotting out frontiers, inventing dynasties, and compelling the nations through which he moved on his charger like a human earthquake or like Antichrist (as he was styled by the Powers of the North), to change their shapes, names, positions, customs, and even their dress....

None the less our fathers (God keep them in His holy Glory), far from hating or fearing him, delighted in the

study of his extraordinary exploits, for all the world as if it were a matter of some hero in a Book of Chivalry or of things which were happening on some other planet, nor for a moment did it cross their minds that he might come hither and attempt the horrors he had wrought in France, Italy, Germany, and other countries. Once a week (twice at best) the post from Madrid arrived in most of the important towns of the Peninsula, bringing a few numbers of the Gazette (which was not, any more than the post, a daily event), and from it the select few learned (supposing that the Gazette happened to mention it) whether there was a state more or less beyond the Pyrenees, or another battle had been fought in which six or eight Kings and

Emperors had taken part, or whether Napoleon happened to be in Milan, Brussels, or Warsaw.... For the rest, our elders went on living, wrapped up in their moth-eaten habits, in God's Peace and Grace, with their Inquisition and their Friars, with their picturesque inequality before the Law, with their privileges, charters, and personal exemptions, with their total lack of municipal or political liberty, governed conjointly by noble Bishops and potent Corregidors (whose respective powers it was far from easy to define since both intermeddled with the temporal and the eternal), and paying tithes, first-fruits, excise, subsidies, compulsory gifts and charities, rents, rates, poll-taxes, royal thirds, gavels, civil fruits, and fifty more tributes whose nomenclature is not now to the purpose.

And here ends all that concerns the present history of the matters military and political of that epoch, since our sole object in touching upon what was then happening in the world has been to come to the conclusion that, in the year of which we treat, the Old Order was still in authority in Spain in all spheres of public and private life, as if, in the midst of all these novelties and upheavals, the Pyrenees had grown into another Great Wall of China.

II. OF HOW FOLK LIVED IN
THOSE DAYS

IN ANDALUSIA, for example (since, in point of fact, it was in a city of Andalusia that what you are about to hear occurred), persons of *position* still rose betimes, visited the Cathedral for Prime Mass, even if it were not a Holiday of Obligation, breakfasting at nine off a fried egg and a cup of chocolate with toast sandwiches; dining, from one to two of the afternoon, off a stew and side-dish, if there were any game, and, if not, off a stew alone; taking the siesta after dinner; then walking out in the country; going to Rosary about twilight in their respective parish churches; taking another chocolate at the Angelus (this time with a biscuit); the bigwigs attending the evening party at the Magistrate's, the Dean's or the local Lord's; returning home at the ringing of the Animas; barring the great door before the tolling of the Curfew; supping off a salad and ragout, if fresh anchovies were not yet come in, and incontinently going to bed with their wives (those that had them), but not, during nine months of the year, before ordering the bed to be warmed....

Happy times, in which our land enjoyed quiet and peaceful possession of all the cobwebs, dust, moth, all the observances, beliefs, traditions, all the uses and abuses sanctified by the ages! Happy times, in which there existed in

human society a variety of classes, prejudices and customs! Happy times, I say, especially for the poets, who might find round every corner an interlude, a farce, a comedy, a drama, a mystery, or an epic, instead of this prosaic uniformity and savourless realism which came to us on the heels of the French Revolution! Happy times, indeed!

But here we are, returning on our tracks! Enough of generalities and circumlocutions: let us enter resolutely upon the history of *The Three-Cornered Hat*.

III. *DO UT DES*

IN THOSE DAYS, then, there stood near a certain city, a famous flour-mill (which exists no longer), situate at about a quarter of a league from the town, between the foot of a gentle hill peopled with orchards of mazard and cherry, and a richly fertile plain which served as a margin (and sometimes as bed) to the intermittent and treacherous river.

For various and diverse reasons, that mill had already for some considerable time been the chosen objective and place of recreation for the most distinguished pleasure-makers of the aforementioned city....In the first place, it was approached by a carriage-road less impassable than the others of that district. In the second place, there was a little flagged court in front of the mill, covered by an enormous vine under which the visitors could enjoy a pleasant coolness in the summer and the warmth of the sunshine in the winter, thanks to the alternate flourishing and falling of the vine-leaves. In the third place, the Miller was a very respectable, discreet, fine fellow, who had what you call "a way with him," and who entertained the worthy Gentlemen who honored him with their company of an evening, with whatever the season provided; now green mazagans, now cherries and mazards, now lettuces in the leaf without seasoning (which are excellent when accompanied by sippets of bread and oil—sippets which the gentlemen undertook to send ahead), now melons, now grapes from that same vine that served them as canopy, now *popcorns* of maize if it was winter-time, and roasted chestnuts, almonds, nuts, and now and then, on very cold evenings, a draught of very decent wine (within doors

7

now and about the fire), to which at Eastertide he would add a few fritters, butter-cakes, or a slice or two of an Al-pujarras ham.

"Was the Miller, then, so wealthy?" you will interrupt me to exclaim, "or was it that his distinguished visitors so far forgot themselves?"

Neither the one nor the other. The Miller had no more than a competence and the gentlemen were the person-ification of delicacy and proper pride. But in times in which men paid upwards of fifty different contributions to Church and State, a fellow as knowing as our Miller found it well worth his while to keep a hold on the good-will of the Aldermen, Canons, Friars, Clerks, and the other folk who could pull wires. And so it was said by not a few that Miller Lucas (for such was our Miller's name), by giving a kindly welcome to all and sundry, was able to put by a very tidy sum at the end of the year.

"Your Worship will let me have the old door from that house you have pulled down," he would say to one. "Your Lordship," he would ask of another, "will order them to give me a rebatement on the subsidy, the excise, or the civil-fruits." "Your Reverence will let me take a few leaves from the Convent garden for my silkworms." "Your Honor will give me a permit to gather a little kindling from Mount *This*." "Your Paternity will write me a line so that they'll allow me to cut a little wood in the pine-forest of *That*." "You must give me a little note, Venerable Sir, so that I can get it free of charge." "This year I can't pay the tax." "I trust the suit will be settled in my favor." "Today I gave a man a thrashing and I think he ought to go to jail for provocation." "Does your Worship happen to have such and such a thing to spare?" "Is your Lordship using...some other thing?" "Can you lend me the mule?" "Will the cart be occupied tomorrow?" "Had I better send for the donkey?"

Our Miller was always finding occasion for little requests of this nature, and the reply was always a generous and impartial "As you wish."

And so you perceive that Miller Lucas was not precisely on the road to ruin.

IV. A WOMAN SEEN FROM
WITHOUT

THE FINAL and perhaps the most potent reason which
the gentry of the City had for frequenting Miller Lucas's
Mill of an evening was . . . that (Clergy and Laity alike,
beginning with the Lord Bishop and his Honor the Corregidor) they could there contemplate at their ease one of
the most lovely, accomplished, and admirable works of
art that ever issued from the hands of God (styled at that
time by Jovellanos and all the frenchified school of our
country, the Supreme Being). . . .

This work of art was entitled "Mistress Frasquita."

I will begin by assuring you that Mistress Frasquita, the lawful wife of Miller Lucas, was a very proper person, and that the illustrious visitors to the Mill were well aware of it. I say more; not one of them betrayed a disposition to regard her with a lustful eye or unsanctified desires. They admired her, certainly, and on occasions they courted her (in the presence of her husband, I suppose), and not only the gallants but the Friars, not only the gownsmen but the Canons, as a prodigy of beauty who did honor to her Creator, and as a demon of sprightliness and coquetry who brought innocent delight to the most melancholy spirits. "She's a lovely creature," the most virtuous Prelate was accustomed to say. "She's a statue of ancient Hellas," observed a learned Counsellor, Corresponding Member of the Historical Academy. "She's the image itself of Eve," asserted the Prior of the Franciscans. "She's a grand girl," exclaimed the Colonel of Militia. "She's a serpent, a siren, a demon!" added the Corregidor. "Nay, she's a good soul, an angel, a darling, a little four-year-old," said all in conclusion as they returned from the Mill, stuffed full of grapes or nuts, and sought their own dull and unromantic firesides.

The little four-year-old, that is, Missis Frasquita, was getting on for thirty. She was above five and a half feet in height, and robust in proportion, perhaps even a trifle heavier than her proud stature warranted. She was like a

11

giant Niobe, though she had borne no children; a Hercules...a she-Hercules; a Roman matron such as you may still see in Trastevere. But the most notable thing about her was the quickness of her movements, the lightsomeness, the animation, the grace of her very ample form. For a statue, as the Academician claimed her to be, she lacked the monumental repose. She could bend like a reed, twirl like a weathercock, dance like a spinning top. Her face was more mobile still, and for that the less sculptural. Its lively charm was made more charming still by no less than five dimples; two on one cheek, another on the other, another (a very little one) not far from the left corner of her laughing lips, and the last (a very big one) right in the middle of her rounded chin. Add to that the roguish looks, the playful winks, and the changing poses of her head which brought such a charm to her conversation, and you may be able to form some idea of that face so full of beauty and humor, so radiant always with happiness and health.

Neither Mistress Frasquita nor Miller Lucas were from Andalusia; she was from Navarre, he from Murcia. He had gone to a certain town of that province at the age of fifteen, as half page, half servant, to the Bishop previous to the one which now held that See. His good patron educated him for the Church, and it was perhaps with an eye to this and in order that he might not lack the wherewithal, that at his death he bequeathed to him the Mill. But

Miller Lucas, who at his Lordship's death had only been ordained to Minor Orders, hung up his surplice there and then and joined for a soldier, being more desirous of adventure and seeing the world than of saying Mass and grinding corn. In 1793 he took part in the campaign of the Western Pyrenees as Orderly to the gallant General Don Ventura Caro; he was present at the attack on Castillo Piñón, and then remained for a long time in the Northern Provinces, where he obtained his discharge. In Estella he made the acquaintance of Mistress Frasquita, who at that time was called simply Frasquita; he fell in love with her,

13

married her, and carried her to Andalusia to the Mill where they were to live in peace and prosperity during the rest of their peregrination through this vale of tears and laughter.

Mistress Frasquita, then, transported from Navarre to this secluded spot, had taken on none of the habits of the Andalusians and remained markedly different from the countrywomen of the district. She dressed with greater simplicity, freedom, and elegance than they, washed herself more frequently, and allowed the sun and air to caress her naked arms and throat. She conformed, up to a certain point, with the dress of the ladies of the period, the dress of Goya's women, the dress of Queen Maria Luisa. The skirt, if not half a pace in width, was no more than a pace, and extremely short, so that it displayed her little feet and the spring of her noble leg. Her bodice she wore cut low and round at the neck in the fashion of Madrid, where she had stayed two months with Miller Lucas on her way from Navarre to Andalusia. Her hair, gathered right up on to the crown of the head, showed off superbly the graceful poise of her head and neck. In her little ears she wore a pair of earrings, and many rings on the slim fingers of her hard but spotless hands. Finally, Mistress Frasquita's voice had the tone and range of some beautiful musical instrument and her laugh was as gay and silvery as a peal of bells on Holy Saturday.

Now for a portrait of Miller Lucas.

V. A MAN SEEN FROM WITHOUT
AND WITHIN

MILLER LUCAS was as ugly as the devil. He had been
so all his life, and now he was about forty years old. None
the less, God can have brought into the world few men
more agreeable and sympathetic. Taken by his liveliness,
his quick wit, and his charm, the late Bishop had begged
him of his parents, who were shepherds, not of souls but
of actual sheep. His Lordship being dead and the boy
having exchanged the Seminary for the Barracks, General

Caro picked him out of his whole army and made him his personal orderly and his servant in the field. After completing his term of service, Miller Lucas found it as easy to subdue the heart of Mistress Frasquita as it had been to win the regard of the General and the Prelate. The young girl of Navarre, who was at that time twenty Aprils old, the apple of the eyes of all the boys in Estella, some of them young men of means, was unable to resist the endless witticisms and gay, sparkling sallies, the monkeyish lovelorn glances, and the continual waggish smile, full of mischief, but full of sweetness too, of this fellow from Murcia. Indeed, such was his effrontery, his gift of the gab, his ready wits, his resourcefulness, his bravery and his charm, that he succeeded in turning the head, not only of the coveted beauty, but of her mother and father as well.

Lucas was at that time, and so continued at the date to which we refer, of little stature (at least as compared with his wife), somewhat round-shouldered, and very dusky. His chin was smooth, his nose and ears large, and he was marked with the smallpox. On the other hand, his mouth was well-shaped and his teeth perfect. You might say that only the husk of the man was uncouth and ugly, that as soon as you penetrated beneath it you began to discover his perfections, and that these perfections began with his teeth. Then came his voice, vibrant, flexible, attractive; at times grave and manly, but sweet and honeyed when

he asked a favor, and always difficult to resist. And then came the things spoken by the voice; all he said was in season, discreet, well-found, persuasive. And lastly, in the soul of Miller Lucas there was courage, loyalty, honor, common sense, desire of knowledge, an understanding natural and acquired of many matters, a profound scorn of fools, whatever their social station, and a certain sense of irony, mockery, and sarcasm which made of him, according to our friend the Academician, a sort of Don Francisco de Quevedo in the rough.

Such, within and without, was Miller Lucas.

VI. THE ACCOMPLISHMENTS
OF OUR COUPLE

WELL, MISTRESS FRASQUITA loved Miller Lucas to madness and held herself to be the happiest woman in the world because *he* adored *her*. They had no children, as we have already learned, and so they had devoted themselves to pampering and petting one another with indescribable care, though this tender solicitude showed none of the cloying sentimentality of almost all childless couples. On the contrary, they treated one another with the directness, light-heartedness, gaiety and trust of children towards their companions in play, who love each other with all their souls without ever confessing as much or even themselves realizing what they feel.

Never before, surely, had the world seen a Miller so neat in his dress and person, or who kept a better table or a home so replete with every comfort, as Miller Lucas. Never was any miller's wife (or for that matter, any queen) surrounded with such attentions, such deference, such consideration, as Mistress Frasquita. And never, surely, did a mill contain such a store of the necessities, conveniences, amenities, distractions, and even the superfluities of life, as the one which is about to serve as theatre for almost all of the present history.

All this was largely due to the fact that Mistress Frasquita, the fair, industrious, healthful woman of Navarre, could, would, and in point of fact did cook, sew, embroider, make sweets, wash, iron, whitewash the house, scour the copper, knead the dough, weave, knit, sing, dance, play the guitar and the castanets, and whist and cribbage, and a vast number of other things to the telling of which there would be no end. And that same result was due no less to the fact that Miller Lucas, could, would, and in point of fact did direct the Mill, till his field, hunt, fish, do the work of carpenter, blacksmith, and mason, help his wife in all the business of the house, read, write, and keep accounts, et cetera, et cetera.

Not to mention his extraordinary accomplishments in matters of pleasure and luxury.

For example, Miller Lucas adored flowers (and so did his wife) and such a past master was he in the art of floriculture that he had succeeded, by means of laborious cross-fertilization, in producing new *varieties*. He was something too of a natural engineer, and had proved as much by constructing a dam, a siphon, and a mill-race which trebled the supply of water to the Mill. He had taught a dog to dance, tamed a snake, made a parrot strike the hour by means of cries in accordance with the time shown by a sun-dial which the Miller had contrived upon a wall, with the result that the parrot struck the hours with perfect precision even on cloudy days and throughout the night.

Finally, the Mill had a kitchen-garden which produced every kind of fruit and vegetable; a pond enclosed in a sort of kiosk of jasmine, in which in summer-time, Miller Lucas and Mistress Frasquita used to bathe; a flower garden; a stove-house or conservatory for exotic plants; a well of drinking water; two donkeys on which the couple rode into town or to the neighboring villages; a hen-house, a dovecote, an aviary, hatcheries for fish and silk-worms, beehives whose bees sucked honey from the jasmines, a wine-press or vat with its appropriate cellar, both in miniature; an oven, loom, forge, carpenter's shop, et cetera, et cetera; all reduced to the compass of an eight-room house and three acres of land and assessed at ten thousand Reals.

VII. THE FOUNDATIONS
OF FELICITY

YES, THE MILLER and his wife adored each other to distraction, and yet, it might have been thought that she loved him more than he her, albeit he was so ugly and she so lovely. I say it because Mistress Frasquita was inclined to be jealous and to ask for explanations when Miller Lucas was late in getting back from town or from the villages to which he went for corn, while Miller Lucas himself actually took pleasure in the attentions which Mistress Frasquita received from the Gentlemen who frequented the mill. He took a pride and pleasure in the fact that she pleased all as much as she pleased him, and although he realized in the bottom of his heart that some of them envied him, coveting her like simple mortals, and would have given something for her to be less of an honest woman than she was, he left her alone for days together without the least concern, and never asked her afterwards what she had been doing or who had been there during his absence. None the less, this did not signify that the love of Miller Lucas was less keen than that of Mistress Frasquita. It signified that he had a greater faith in her virtue than she in his; it signified that he had the advantage of her in penetration and well knew the degree to which he was loved and how much his wife respected herself; and it signified chiefly that Miller Lucas was in every point a man, a man like Shakespeare's men, of few but fixed emotions, incapable of doubt; a man who must trust or die, love or slay; who admitted no degrees or middle paths between supreme happiness and the total extinction of joy.

He was, in fine, a Murcian Othello in rope-sandals and a cap, in the first act of a possible tragedy.

But why these lugubrious notes in a music so merry? Why these ominous flashes in so serene an atmosphere? Why these melodramatic postures in a plain domestic scene?

You shall hear, without more ado.

VIII. THE MAN WITH
THE THREE-CORNERED HAT

IT WAS TWO O'CLOCK of an October afternoon. The Cathedral bell was ringing to Vespers, which is as much as to say that all the principal persons of the town had already dined.

Canons were making their way to the Choir and Laymen to the bedrooms to take the siesta, especially those who by reason of office (for example, the town Authorities) had spent the whole morning at work.

And so it was a matter for surprise that at such an hour (a most unsuitable one, moreover, for taking a walk, since the day was still excessively hot) there should leave the City on foot and attended only by one Bailiff, its illustrious Corregidor, a man to be confused with no other person either by day or by night, not only because of the enormous size of his three-cornered hat and the splendor of his scarlet cloak, but also because of the peculiarity of his grotesque carriage.

There are people, not a few, still surviving who could speak out of a full knowledge of that scarlet cloak and the three-cornered hat. Ourselves, among the number, as well as all those born in that City during the last days of the reign of Don Fernando VII, can remember to have seen hanging from a nail, the unique adornment of a dis-

mantled wall in the ruined tower of the house once occupied by his Lordship (a tower given over at this time to the innocent games of his grandchildren), those two antiquated articles of apparel, the cape and the hat—the black hat on top, the red cape beneath—forming a kind of bogy of Absolutism, a kind of sacred relic of the Corregidor, a kind of retrospective caricature of his authority, designed in charcoal and sanguine, like so many others, for us little Constitutionalists of 1837, who were in the habit of meeting there; in short, a kind of scarecrow, which in other days had acted as a *scare-man*, and which still frightens *me* today when I recall that I myself helped to jeer at the thing, carried in procession through that historic City in Carnival time, at the end of a sweep's brush, or serving as a comic disguise for the idiot who could best make the crowd laugh. Poor Principle of Authority! This is the pass to which we have brought you, we who are never tired of invoking you today!

As for that matter of the Corregidor's grotesque carriage, it consisted (so they say) in the fact that he was heavy in the shoulder, heavier even than Miller Lucas; to put it in a word, almost hunchbacked; in height below the average; a puny figure of a man and of poor health, bowlegged and with a manner of walking which was all his own,—a rocking of himself from one side to another and backwards and forwards which can only be described by the absurd formula that he seemed to be lame in both legs at once. On the other hand (tradition adds), his face was regular though somewhat creased and crinkled by reason of an almost complete lack of teeth. He was dusky—a greenish olive, like almost all the sons of the Castiles; in his large, dark eyes you might often see a flash of anger, of tyranny, or of lust. His fine shrewd features were expressive not so much of personal bravery as of a crafty malice capable of anything, together with a certain self-satisfied air, half aristocratic, half dissolute, which revealed that the man had been, in his remote youth, very agreeable and attractive to the women, in spite of his legs and his hunch.

Don Eugenio de Zúñiga y Ponce de León (for such was his Honor's name), was born in Madrid of an illustrious family. He was at this time close upon the fifty-fifth year of his age and the fourth of his office of Corregidor of the City of our story, whereof, soon after his first arrival, he had married the principal Lady of whom we shall have more to say hereafter.

Don Eugenio's stockings (the only detail of his clothing besides his shoes, which the great scarlet cloak left to view) were white, and the shoes black, with gold buckles. But when the heat of the open country compelled him to un-muffle himself, it became evident that he wore a great cravat of cambric, a dove-colored waistcoat of twilled silk richly brocaded with a raised pattern of green sprigs, short breeches of black silk, an enormous coat of the same stuff as the waistcoat, a sword with a steel guard, a stick with tassels, and a pair of straw-colored shammy gloves which he never put on, but grasped as if they were a symbol of office.

The Bailiff who followed the Corregidor at twenty paces' distance, had the name of Weasel, and he was the spit and image of his name. Lean and nimble, with eyes that darted backwards and forwards and right and left all the time he was walking, with a long neck, a small, repellent face, hands like a pair of flogging faggots, he seemed to have been created expressly for the punishment of criminals—the ferret to smell them out, the rope to bind them, and the lash to scourge them.

The first Corregidor to set eyes on him had exclaimed without further formalities: "You're the Bailiff for me." And he had been so already for four of them.

He was forty-eight years old and wore a three-cornered hat much smaller than his Master's (since *his*, we must repeat, was of abnormal size). His cape was black, as were his stockings and the rest of his dress; he carried a stick without tassels and had a kind of skewer for a sword.

This black scarecrow appeared to be the shadow of his resplendent Master.

IX. GEE UP, DONKEY!

EVERYWHERE, when the great man and his pendant passed, the laborers left their work, raised their hats, and bowed, from fear rather than respect; after which they said among themselves, *sotto voce:*

"The Corregidor's going early today to see Mistress Frasquita!"

"Early...and alone!" added some of the others who had always been accustomed to see him take that walk in company with various other persons.

"Hark you, Manuel!" a village-woman asked of her husband who was carrying her on the crupper of his beast. "Why is the Corregidor going alone this afternoon to see that Navarrese woman?" And at the same time she tickled him in the ribs by way of emphasis.

"Now don't go getting wrong ideas, Josefa," cried the good man. "Mistress Frasquita wouldn't *think* ..."

"I don't say she would. But that doesn't mean that the Corregidor wouldn't think of falling in love with her. I've heard say that one of the folk that go to those randies at the mill is up to no good, and *that* one is this gentleman from Madrid who is so partial to a petticoat."

"And how do you know he's partial to a petticoat?" enquired the husband.

"I don't speak for myself...! Corregidor though he is,

30

he would think twice before he tried his flatteries on me!"

Now the good woman, as it happened, was as ugly as she could be.

"Now look here, my girl; you let them alone!" answered he whom we have called Manuel. "Miller Lucas is not the sort of man to stand it. He can show a pretty spirit, can Miller Lucas, when he gets angry."

"Still, be that as it may, he doesn't seem to mind!" remarked Josefa, twitching her snout.

"Miller Lucas is the proper sort," answered the villager, "and the proper sort doesn't hold with a certain sort of goings-on."

"Well, have it your own way! Let them be! But if I was Mistress Frasquita…!"

"Gee up, Donkey!" shouted the husband, by way of changing the conversation.

And the donkey set off at a trot and drowned the rest of the conversation.

WHILE this discussion was going on among the laborers who had saluted the Corregidor, Mistress Frasquita was carefully sprinkling and sweeping the little flagged court which served as porch or precinct to the Mill, and was setting out half-a-dozen chairs under the thickest part of the vine-arbor into which Miller Lucas had climbed and where he was now gathering the finest bunches and arranging them artistically in a basket.

"Yes, Frasquita," came Miller Lucas's voice from up in the arbor. "The Corregidor is in love with you in a very evil fashion."

"I told you so some time ago!" answered Frasquita. "Well, let him love! Look out, Lucas; don't you fall."

"Never worry; I've got a good hold....And there's another of them..."

"Look here, say no more about it," she broke in. "I know well enough who's fond of me and who is not. I only wish I knew as well why you're not fond of me."

"Because you're so ugly, of course!" answered Miller Lucas.

"Ugly and all, I could climb up there and pitch you down head first."

"More likely you wouldn't get down again till I'd eaten you alive."

"That's it! And when my young men came up and saw us up here, they'd say we were a couple of monkeys."

"Well, they'd be quite right. Don't I look like a monkey with this hump of mine; and you're a saucy little monkey yourself."

"It's a very nice hump!"

"Then the Corregidor's must be a nicer one still, because it's bigger than mine."

"Come, come, Mr. Lucas! Not so much jealousy, please!"

"I jealous of that old skunk? Nothing of the kind. I'm very glad he loves you."

"And why, pray?"

"Because where there's sin there's penance. You don't have to love him at all, and meanwhile I'm the real Corregidor of the City."

"I like your conceit! Well, you'd better remember that I might come to love him. Stranger things have happened in the world."

"That wouldn't trouble me much, either."

"And why not?"

"Because then you wouldn't be you any longer; and if you stopped being what you are, or what I think you are, damn me if I'd care if the Devil himself ran away with you."

"Well, what would you do then?"

"Me? How am I to know? Because then, you see, I

33

should be different—not the same man as I am now; and so how can I tell what I should think about it?"

"Why would you be different?" Mistress Frasquita insisted boldly, stopping her sweeping, and standing, hands on hips, to gaze up into the vine.

Miller Lucas scratched his head as if he hoped to scratch some profounder thought out of it. When at last he spoke it was with a greater seriousness than usual:

"I should be different, because now I am a man who trusts you as he trusts himself, and whose whole life is in that faith. Consequently, if I ceased to trust you, I should either die or change into a new man; I should live in a different way; it would be as if I had just been born; I should have a different mind. I have no idea what I should do with you. Perhaps I should burst out laughing and turn my back on you. Perhaps I shouldn't even know you. Perhaps...! But Lord, what a funny way of amusing ourselves, getting into a state over nothing. What do we care if all the Corregidors fall in love with you? Aren't you my Frasquita?"

"Of course I am, you great heathen," she answered, laughing heartily. "I'm your Frasquita and you're my own ugly Lucas, cleverer than everyone else put together, better than good bread-and-butter, dearer...well, you'll see how dear when you come down from that vine. Yes, you'll get more pinches and punches than you've got hairs

34

on your head. But hush! What's this? There's the Corregidor coming all by himself. And how early! There's something in this. You were right, seemingly!"

"Well, don't check him, and don't tell him I'm up here. He thinks you're alone. He thinks he's caught me at my siesta and he's going to pop the question. What a joke! I'm going to hear what he's got to say."

So saying, Miller Lucas reached down the basket to his wife.

"Not a bad idea!" she exclaimed, bursting out laughing again. "The old devil! Fancy me catching a Corregidor! But here he comes. Weasel will have followed him; not a doubt of it; and now he'll be sitting in the shade in the gully. What a nonsensical business, to be sure! Mind you keep well hidden in those vine-leaves; we're going to have the laugh of our lives."

And so saying, the lovely creature started singing the Fandango which by this time came as natural to her as the songs of her own land.

XI. THE BOMBARDMENT
OF PAMPELUNA

"GOD guard you, Frasquita," said the Corregidor, dropping his voice, as he appeared on tiptoe under the arbor.

"You're very good, my Lord!" she replied in the most natural voice in the world and made him a thousand curtsies. "How is it you're here so soon, and on a hot day like this too? Come, let your Honor take a seat! It's nice and fresh here. How is it your Honor hasn't waited for the other gentlemen? This evening we are expecting my Lord Bishop in person. He promised my Lucas to come and try the first grapes from the vine here. And how does your Honor? And how is your Honor's Lady?"

The Corregidor felt himself somewhat confused. It seemed to him a dream that his hopes should have been realized and that he should have found Mistress Frasquita alone; a dream, or perhaps a trap set for him by an envious fate to hurl him into the pit of disappointment.

And so he contented himself with replying: "It is not so early as you think. It must be half-past three."

At that moment the parrot gave a scream.

"It is a quarter-past-two," said Frasquita, gazing fixedly at the old man.

The culprit held his peace and made no further attempt to defend himself.

"What about Lucas? Is he asleep?" he asked after a moment. (We must here remark that the Corregidor, like all who have lost their teeth, spoke with a loose, whistling utterance as if he were in the act of eating his own lips.)

"He is, indeed," answered Mistress Frasquita. "At this time of day he sleeps wherever it happens to take him, even if it's on the edge of a precipice."

"Well, look here! Let him sleep!" exclaimed the old man, turning even paler than before. "And you, my dear Frasquita, listen to me...hark ye...come here....Sit you down here, beside me. I have much to say to you."

"Certainly, my Lord," replied the Miller's wife, grasping a low chair and placing it in front of the Corregidor, at a polite distance from his own. And having seated herself, Frasquita threw one leg over the other, leaned forward, propped an elbow upon her crossed knee and her fresh, lovely face in one of her hands; and thus, with her head a little on one side, a smile on her lips, the five dimples in action, and her serene eyes fixed on the Corregidor, she awaited his Honor's declaration. She might have been compared to Pampeluna expecting a bombardment.

The poor man tried to speak, but remained open-mouthed, dazzled by that superb loveliness, by the brilliance of those charms; yes, dazzled by the whole awe-inspiring woman, with her alabaster skin, her luscious body, her

37

clean and laughing mouth, her blue unfathomable eyes—
a creation, it seemed, of the brush of Rubens.

"Frasquita," murmured at last the King's delegate in
fainting accents, while, bathed in perspiration, his with-
ered face, standing out against his hunched shoulders, expressed an intense anguish. "Frasquita!"

"That is my name," she answered. "What then?"

"What you wish…" replied the old man with extreme
tenderness.

"What I wish," said the Miller's wife, "your Honor
knows already. I wish you to nominate as Secretary of the
Municipal Council a nephew of mine in Estella, so that
he can come away from those mountains, where he is in a
very bad way."

"I have told you, Frasquita, that it is out of the question.
The present Secretary…"

"Is a thief, a drunkard, and a beast!"

"I know. But he happens to be in the good books of the
Perpetual Aldermen and I cannot nominate another with-
out the concurrence of the Corporation. On the contrary,
I should risk…"

"Risk! Risk! And what is there that we of this house,
down to the very cats, would not risk to please your
Honor?"

"Is that the price of your love?" stammered the Corregidor.

"No, Sir. I love your Honor free of charge."

"Don't call me *your Honor*, woman. Call me plain *you*, or whatever you like.... Then you promise to love me! Eh?"

"Haven't I told you that I love you already?"

"But...!"

"There's no *but* about it. You'll see what a fine, honest fellow my nephew is."

"Ah, Frasquita! It's you, my dear, that are fine."

"So you like me?"

"I like you? There's not a woman to compare with you."

"Look, then! There's nothing sham about me," answered Mistress Frasquita, rolling up the sleeve of her bodice and showing the rest of her arm, an arm worthy of a caryatid and whiter than a white lily.

"Like you?" pursued the Corregidor. "By day, by night, at every moment, wherever I am, I think of nothing but you."

"What? Don't you like her Ladyship, then?" asked Mistress Frasquita with a mock sympathy that would have made a hypochondriac laugh. "What a pity! My Lucas told me that it was a pleasure to see her and speak to her when he went to mend the clock in the bedroom for you, she is such a fine lady, so good, so affable in her manner."

"Not altogether! Not altogether!" murmured the Corregidor with a touch of bitterness.

"On the other hand, some folk have told me," proceeded the Miller's wife, "that she is very ill-humored and jealous, and rules you with a rod of iron."

"Not altogether, woman," repeated Don Eugenio de Zúñiga y Ponce de León, turning somewhat red. "Not altogether, and yet perhaps a little! My Lady has her tantrums, no doubt; but there's some difference between tantrums and ruling me with a rod of iron. After all, I am the Corregidor."

"Anyhow, do you love her, or do you not?"

"I'll tell you. I love her much, or, to put it better, I did love her till I met you. But since I saw you, I don't know what has come over me...she herself sees that something has come over me. All I can tell you is that nowadays if I pat my wife's cheek, for instance, it gives me the same feelings as if I patted my own. But to touch your hand, your arm, your chin, your waist, I would give all I have in the world."

And so saying, the Corregidor tried to possess himself of the bare arm which Mistress Frasquita in actual fact was stroking under his very eyes. But she, without disturbing herself, reached out her hand, touched his Honor's breast with the peaceful violence and irresistible firmness of an elephant's trunk, and pushed him over, chair and all.

"Holy Virgin!" cried the wicked creature, laughing consumedly. "The chair must have been broken."

"What's all this?" cried Miller Lucas at the same moment, pushing his ugly face out of the vine-leaves.

The Corregidor, still sprawling on the ground, face upwards, gazed in unspeakable terror at this man hovering in the air above him, face downwards.

You might have said that his Honor was the Devil, defeated, not by Saint Michael, but by another devil from Hell.

"What is it? Why his Honor tipped up his chair, tried to rock himself, and tumbled over."

"Jesus, Mary and Joseph!" cried the Miller in his turn. "And has your Honor hurt himself? Shall I fetch some water and vinegar?"

"It's nothing! It's nothing!" said the Corregidor, scrambling up as well as he could. And he added, under his breath but so that Mistress Frasquita could hear: "I'll pay you out for this."

"Anyhow, his Honor has saved my life," replied Miller Lucas, who was still up in the top of the arbor. "Just fancy, wife; I was sitting up here looking over the grapes, when I fell asleep just as I was, on this crisscross of posts and branches full of holes as big as my body. So you see, if his Honor's tumble hadn't woken me in time, I should have cracked my crown on the flags down there this very afternoon."

"Eh? What?" replied the Corregidor. "Why then, I'm glad, man; I tell you I'm glad that I tumbled over."

"Yes, I'll pay you out for this," he concluded, turning to the Miller's wife. And he uttered the words with such an expression of concentrated fury that Mistress Frasquita began to look serious.

She saw clearly that at first, believing that the Miller had heard everything, the Corregidor was afraid, but that, being soon convinced that he had heard nothing (for the calm cunning of Miller Lucas might well have deceived the sharpest), he began to indulge his anger to the full and to imagine schemes of vengeance.

"Now, down you come from there, and help me to tidy up his Honor. He's covered with dust," she cried to her husband.

And while Miller Lucas was climbing down, she said to the Corregidor, as she beat his coat and more than once his ears with her apron: "The poor dear has heard nothing. He was sleeping like a log."

More than the phrases themselves, the fact that Frasquita had dropped her voice to say them produced a miraculous effect.

"You wicked creature! You hussy!" babbled Don Eugenio de Zúñiga y Ponce de León, growling still, but with a watering mouth.

"Your Honor won't remember this against me?" coaxed Mistress Frasquita.

The Corregidor, observing that severity paid, did his

best to look furious; but, meeting her seductive laugh and her divine eyes shining with supplication, he melted on the spot.

"It depends on you, my love!" he slobbered, and the total lack of teeth was more than ever noticeable in his whistling utterance.

At that moment Miller Lucas dropped to the ground out of the arbor.

XII. TITHES AND FIRSTFRUITS

WHEN the Corregidor had been restored to his chair, the Miller's wife shot a rapid glance at her husband, and found him not merely as undisturbed as usual but ready to burst with suppressed laughter. She threw him a kiss, snatching the first moment when Don Eugenio was not looking; and to Don Eugenio she said in a siren voice that Cleopatra herself might have envied:

"Now your Honor's going to try my grapes."

Then the lovely creature might have been seen (and so would I paint her, if I had the brush of a Titian) standing before the dazzled Corregidor, fresh, superb, provocative, with her noble figure, her fine height, her naked arms raised above her head and a translucent grape-bunch in either hand. Then, between an irresistible smile and a beseeching glance in which there was a flicker of fear, she said to him:

"My Lord the Bishop has not tasted them yet. They're the first to be gathered this year."

She stood there like a great Pomona offering fruits to a country deity—to a Satyr, in fact.

Thereupon, at the far end of the flagged court, there came into view the venerable Bishop of the Diocese, accompanied by the Counsellor Academician and two Canons of advanced years, and followed by his Secretary, two body-servants and two pages.

His Lordship paused for a moment before a picture at once so comical and so lovely; finally he remarked, speaking with the leisured utterance proper to Prelates of the time:

"Fifthly…to pay tithes and firstfruits to the Church of God, so Christian doctrine teaches us; but you, my Lord Corregidor, are not content to administer the tithes, but are trying, it seems, to devour the firstfruits."

"My Lord the Bishop!" exclaimed the Miller and his wife, leaving the Corregidor and running to kiss the Prelate's ring.

"God reward your Lordship for deigning to honor this poor hovel," said Miller Lucas in accents of sincere veneration as he gave the first kiss.

"My most gracious Lord," exclaimed Mistress Frasquita as she kissed after him, "God bless you and preserve you to me longer than He preserved my Lucas's master to him."

"What can I do, when you give me your blessing instead of asking me for mine?" replied the kindly Bishop, laughing heartily. And raising two fingers he blessed Mistress Frasquita and then the rest of the company.

"Here are the firstfruits, my Lord," said the Corregidor, taking a bunch of grapes from the hands of the Miller's wife and presenting it courteously to the Bishop. "I had not yet tried them."

As he pronounced these words the Corregidor shot a

46

quick, cynical glance at the superb beauty of the Miller's wife.

"Not however because they were green like those in the fable!" observed the Academician.

"Those in the fable," remarked the Bishop, "were not green, my Learned Friend, but out of reach of the fox."

Perhaps neither had intended to allude to the Corregidor, but both remarks, as it happened, were so applicable to what had just happened there, that Don Eugenio de Zúñiga turned livid with anger. "Which is to call me a fox," he said, as he kissed the Prelate's ring.

"*Tu dixisti!*" replied the latter, with the courteous severity of a saint, which, in effect, they say he was. "*Excusatio non petita, accusatio manifesta. Qualis vir, talis oratio.* But *satis jam dictum, nullus ultra sit sermo;* or, what amounts to the same thing, let us leave Latin and inspect these famous grapes."

And he took one grape only from the bunch which the Corregidor was offering him.

"They are very good!" he exclaimed, holding up the grape to the light and then handing it to his Secretary. "I am sorry that they don't agree with me."

The Secretary likewise studied the grape, made a gesture of courteous admiration and handed it to one of the body-servants.

The body-servant repeated the action of the Bishop and the gesture of the Secretary, going so far as to smell the grape, and then...placed it in the basket with scrupulous care, at the same time remarking to the company in a low voice:

"His Lordship is fasting."

Miller Lucas, who had watched the progress of the grape, stealthily took it, and, when nobody was looking, ate it.

After this, everyone sat down. They spoke of the season, which was very dry, although the first storm of autumn (the scourge of Saint Francis, as they call it) had already occurred. For a while they discussed the probability of a new war between Napoleon and Austria, and expressed the firm belief that the Imperial troops would never invade Spanish territory. The Counsellor complained of the restless and calamitous epoch in which they lived and envied the tranquil times of their parents (as their parents had envied those of their grandparents). The parrot struck five, and, at a sign from the Reverend Bishop, the smaller of the pages went off to the episcopal coach (which was waiting in the same gully as the Bailiff), and returned with a magnificent pastry-cake, sprinkled with salt, which had come out of the oven hardly an hour ago. A table was set in the middle of the company; the cake was quartered; Miller Lucas and Mistress Frasquita were given their appropriate share, despite their energetic resistance, and a truly democratic equality reigned for half an hour beneath those vine-leaves which filtered the last splendors of the setting sun.

XIII. SAID THE
JACKDAW TO THE CROW

AN HOUR and a half later all the illustrious company was back again in the City.

The Lord Bishop and his *family* had arrived some time ahead of the rest, thanks to the coach, and were already *in residence*, where we will leave them to their devotions.

The distinguished Counsellor (who was very lean) and the two Canons (each more plump and dignified than the other), accompanied the Corregidor as far as the door of the Town Hall (where his Honor said that he had some work to do) and then made their way towards their respective homes, steering by the stars like navigators or groping round corners like blind men; since the night had already closed in, the moon was not yet risen, and the public lighting (like that other Enlightenment of the period) existed only in the divine mind.

On the other hand, it was not uncommon to see a lantern or torch flitting now and then along the street, borne by some respectful servant who was lighting his stately master and mistress to the customary party or to pay a call on certain of their relatives.

At the bars of almost every low window was to be seen (or, to speak more accurately, to be scented) a black and

silent shape. It was a lover, who, hearing footsteps, had paused for a moment in his love-making.

"We're a lot of tomfools," said the Counsellor and the Canons as they passed. "What will they think at home when they see us returning at such hours?"

"And what will the folk say who meet us in the street, like this, after seven of the night, slinking along like brigands under cover of darkness?"

"We shall have to turn over a new leaf."

"We shall! And yet, that delightful Mill!"

"My wife can't stomach the Mill," said the Academician in a tone that betrayed considerable fear of the forthcoming conjugal skirmish.

"And what about my niece?" exclaimed one of the Canons, who was clearly a Penitentiary. "My niece says that priests have no business to pay visits to gossips…"

"And yet," interrupted his companion, who was a Prebend, "nothing could be more innocent than what goes on there."

"I should think so when the very Lord Bishop himself is one of the party."

"And then, gentlemen, at our age…" replied the Penitentiary. "Yesterday I turned seventy-five."

"The thing's obvious," answered the Prebendary. "But let us talk of something else. How fine Mistress Frasquita was this evening!"

"Oh, as for that, she's a fine woman as fineness goes!"
said the Counsellor, affecting a certain impartiality.

"A very fine woman," reiterated the Penitentiary into
his muffler.

"And if you don't think so," added the Prebendary,
"ask the Corregidor."

"The poor man's in love with her."

"I verily believe he is," exclaimed the Penitentiary.

"Not a doubt of it," added the Corresponding Academician. "Well, gentlemen, this is my best way home. A
very good night to you!"

"Good night!" answered the Capitulars, and they continued a few steps in silence.

Then the Prebendary dug the Penitentiary in the ribs.
"He's in love with the Miller's wife too," he murmured.

"So it would appear," replied the latter, stopping at the
door of his house. "And what a gross fellow he is! Well,
till tomorrow, friend! I trust the grapes will agree with
you."

"Till tomorrow, if God wills. A very good night to
you!"

"God send us a good night," prayed the Penitentiary,
already in his porch which, by the same token, held a lantern and a figure of our Lady.

He raised the knocker.

Once alone in the street, the other Canon (who was

broader than he was long and rolled in his walk) went slowly on his way towards his house...and remarked, thinking no doubt of his colleague:

"And you too are in love with Mistress Frasquita! And the truth is," he added after a moment, "that, as fineness goes, she's a fine woman."

XIV. WEASEL'S ADVICE

·MEANWHILE the Corregidor had gone up into the Town Hall, accompanied by Weasel, with whom, in the Council Chamber, he was for some time engaged in a conversation somewhat more familiar than sorted with a person of his quality and office.

"Let your Honor trust a dog that knows the sport," the Bailiff was saying. "Mistress Frasquita is crazy about your Honor, and all that your Honor has just told me shows me as much, clearer than that light…" and he pointed to a lamp which hardly illuminated an eighth of the room.

"I am not as sure as you, Weasel," answered Don Eugenio, sighing languidly.

"Then I don't know why! But, if you're not, let us speak frankly. Your Honor (may I be pardoned for saying so) has a certain blemish…haven't you?"

"Well, yes," answered the Corregidor. "But Miller Lucas has one too. He is more hunchbacked than I."

"Much more! Very much more! Out of all comparison! But on the other hand (and this is what I was coming to), your Honor has a face of very good appearance, what you call a handsome face, while Miller Lucas is fit to burst with ugliness."

The Corregidor smiled with a certain loftiness.

"Besides," pursued the Bailiff, "Mistress Frasquita is ready to throw herself out of the window to get that nomination for her nephew."

"As to that, I agree. That nomination is my one hope."

"Then get to work, your Honor! I have told you my plan already. The only thing left to do is to set it going this very night."

"I have often told you that I am not in need of advice," cried Don Eugenio, suddenly remembering that he was talking with an inferior.

"I thought your Honor asked me for it," stammered Weasel.

"Don't answer back."

Weasel touched his hat.

"So you were saying," pursued Don Eugenio, mild once more, "that all this might be arranged this very night? Well, look here, my boy; I like the idea of it. What the devil! It's the quickest way of escaping from this cruel uncertainty."

Weasel kept silence.

The Corregidor went to the writing-table and wrote a few lines on a sheet of stamped paper, set his own stamp on it, and then put it away in his pocket.

"The nephew's nomination is complete," he said, taking a pinch of snuff. "Tomorrow I will put myself right with the Aldermen... and either they will confirm it or there will be another siege of St. Quentin. Isn't that the way to do it?"

"That's the way! That's the way!" exclaimed the delighted Weasel, putting a claw into the Corregidor's snuff box and snatching a pinch. "That's the way! Your Honor's predecessor didn't beat about the bush either. I remember once..."

"Stop your chattering," said the Corregidor, giving a smack to the thieving hand. "My predecessor was an ass if he had you for a Bailiff. To business! You told me just now that Miller Lucas's Mill comes within the boundary of the next Village and not of this town. Now, are you sure of that?"

"Quite sure! The City boundary ends at the gully where I sat this afternoon waiting till your Honor...Devil take me! If *I'd* been in your place..."

"Enough, saucy fellow!" cried Don Eugenio; and, taking a half-sheet of paper, he wrote a note, sealed it, folded it, and handed it to Weasel. "Here is the letter," he said, "which you asked me for, to the Mayor of the Village. You will explain to him by word of mouth everything that he must do. You see, I am following your plan precisely. And woe betide you if you land me in a blind alley."

"Never fear," answered Weasel. "Master Juan López has cause to be careful, and, as soon as he sees your Honor's signature, he'll do everything I tell him. He owes at

least fifteen hundred bushels of grain to the State Granary and another fifteen hundred to the Charity Store; this last against all law, for it's not as if he was a widow or a poor laborer to receive corn without paying interest in kind. He's nothing but a gambler, a drunkard, a brazen-faced villain, always after a petticoat, the scandal of the Village. And that man's a person in authority! Well, such is life!"

"I've told you to be quiet. You're disturbing me," blustered the Corregidor. "Well," he added, changing his tone, "to business! It is a quarter past seven. The first thing you must do is to go to the house and tell her Ladyship not to wait for me either for supper or after. Tell her I shall be working here tonight till Curfew and shall then be going on patrol with you, to see if we can catch certain miscreants.... In short, tell her something that will make her go peacefully to bed. On your way, tell the other Bailiff to bring me some supper. I won't venture myself into her Ladyship's presence this evening, because she knows me so well that she's quite capable of reading my thoughts. Order the cook to give me some of those fritters that were made today, and tell Johnny to get me from the tavern, when no one is looking, half a pint of white wine. Then off you go to the Village, where you can very well be by half-past eight."

"I'll be there at eight prompt," exclaimed Weasel.

"Don't contradict me," growled the Corregidor, remembering once again who he was.

Weasel touched his hat.

"We have said," continued the other, human once more, "that you will be at the Village promptly at eight. From the Village to the Mill will be...it will be, I suppose, half a league."

"A short one!"

"Don't interrupt me."

The Bailiff touched his hat again.

"A short one," pursued the Corregidor. "In consequence, at ten.... Shall we say at ten?"

"Before ten! At half-past nine your Honor will be quite safe in calling at the Mill."

"Fellow! Don't tell *me* what I have to do. Now as to *your* place...suppose you are..."

"I shall be everywhere. But my headquarters will be the gully. Ah! I'd almost forgotten! Let your Honor go on foot, and don't take a lantern."

"Again! What the devil do I want with your advice, man? Do you imagine it's the first time I have done this sort of thing?"

"Pardon, your Honor. Ah! Another thing. Don't let your Honor call at the great door which gives on the court where the arbor is, but at the little door there is above the mill-race..."

"There is another door above the mill-race? Why, look you, that's a thing that never occurred to me."

"Yes, my Lord. The little door by the mill-race leads straight into the couple's bedroom, and Miller Lucas never goes in or out by it. So that, although he came back unexpectedly..."

"I follow. I follow. Don't deafen me, man."

"Lastly, be sure your Honor slips away before dawn. Dawn now is at six o'clock."

"More useless advice. At five I shall be back home. But

60

we have talked too much already.... Out of my presence!"

"Then, good luck, my Lord," exclaimed the Bailiff, reaching out a hand to the Corregidor and at the same time gazing at the ceiling.

The Corregidor placed in the hand one peseta and Weasel vanished as if by magic.

"S'life," muttered the old man after a moment, "if I haven't forgotten to tell that chatterer that they must bring me a pack of cards as well! With a pack of cards I could have amused myself till half-past nine trying to get out that solitaire."

XV. PROSAIC FAREWELL

IT WOULD be nine of the same night when Miller Lucas and Mistress Frasquita, having despatched all the business of the Mill and the house, sat down to sup off a bowl of chicory salad, a pound of meat garnished with tomatoes, and a few of the grapes which remained in the aforementioned basket; the whole washed down with a drop of wine and a flood of laughter at the expense of the Corregidor. After which the pair glanced smilingly at one another as if well content with God and themselves, and exclaimed between a couple of yawns which revealed all the peace and tranquillity of their hearts:

"Well, to bed, Sir. There's another day tomorrow."

At that very moment two loud and vigorous knocks rang upon the great door of the Mill.

Husband and wife stared at each other thunderstruck. Never before had there come a knocking at their door at such an hour.

"I'll go and see," said the fearless wife, moving towards the court.

"Stop! This is my job," exclaimed Miller Lucas with such dignity that Mistress Frasquita let him pass. "I've told you not to go," he added sternly, seeing that the obstinate creature wished to follow him.

She obeyed and remained indoors.

"Who is it?" called Miller Lucas from halfway across the court.

"The Law," answered a voice through the great door.

"What Law?"

"The Law of the Village. Open, Sir, to the Mayor."

Miller Lucas had meanwhile applied an eye to a certain peephole cunningly contrived in the door, and had recognized by the light of the moon the clownish Bailiff of the neighboring Village.

"Why don't you say 'Open to this drunkard of a Bailiff?'" answered the Miller, drawing the bolt.

"It's all the same," replied the voice outside. "Haven't I his Honor's written Order? Good evening to you, Miller Lucas," added the Bailiff as he came in. His voice was less official now, deeper and thicker, as if he already felt himself another man.

"God keep you, Tony!" replied the Miller. "Let's see what this Order is! Señor Juan López might have chosen a more suitable hour for business with honest folk. But I expect it's your fault. You've had a drink or two on the way, seemingly. Will you take another?"

"No, Sir: there's no time for anything. You've got to follow me at once. Read the Order."

"Follow you?" exclaimed Miller Lucas, going into the mill when he had taken the paper. "Here, Frasquita! A light!"

Mistress Frasquita put down something she was hold-ing and unhooked the oil-lamp. Miller Lucas cast a rapid glance at the object that his wife had put down and recog-nized his bell-mouth, to wit, an enormous blunderbuss which carried bullets up to half a pound. Then the Miller turned on his wife a look full of gratitude and affection.

"You're a wonder," he said to her, taking her face in his hands.

Mistress Frasquita, pale and calm as a marble statue, lifted the lamp which she held in two fingers, without the least tremor of her pulse.

"Come! Read it!" she answered coldly.

The Order ran as follows:

For the better service of His Majesty the King Our Lord (Q.D.G.), I give notice to Lucas Fernández, miller, of this neighborhood, that, as soon as he shall receive this order, he shall present himself before my authority without excuse or pretext; warning him that, the mat-ter being confidential, he communicate it to no one; all this subject to the proper penalties in case of disobedience.

JUAN LÓPEZ, Mayor.

And there was a cross in place of the signature.

"Look here! What's this?" Miller Lucas asked the Bail-iff. "What's the meaning of this Order?"

"I don't know," replied the rustic, a man of some thirty

65

years, whose face (a sharp, crooked one it was, like a thief's or a cut-throat's) spoke ill for his sincerity. "I think it's about investigating something to do with witchcraft or false money. But the thing doesn't concern you. They're simply calling you as a witness or an expert. In fact, I haven't gone into the particulars. Señor Juan López will tell you the ins and outs of it."

"Right!" exclaimed the Miller. "Tell him I'll come to-morrow."

"Oh no, Sir! You've got to come now, without losing a minute. Those are the orders I had from the Mayor."

There was a moment's silence. Mistress Frasquita's eyes were flashing; Miller Lucas kept his on the ground as if he were seeking something.

"At least you'll give me the time to go to the stable and saddle a donkey," he exclaimed at last, raising his head.

"Donkey? The devil I will!" replied the Bailiff. "Surely a man can go half a league on foot! It's a beautiful night; there's a moon!"

"Yes, the moon's risen, I know. But I suffer from swollen feet."

"Very well, then, don't let us waste time. I'll help you to saddle the beast."

"Hollo! Hollo! Are you frightened that I'll escape?"

"I'm frightened of nothing, Miller Lucas," answered Tony, as cool as a corpse. "I am the Law."

So saying, he *ordered arms*, and by so doing revealed the musket which he carried under his cloak.

"Look here, Tony," said the Miller's wife. "As you're going to the stable, in the exercise of your duty, do me the favor to saddle the other donkey too."

"Why?" asked the Miller.

"For me. I'm going with you."

"You can't, Mistress Frasquita," objected the Bailiff. "My orders are to fetch your husband, nothing more, and to prevent you following him. It's as much as my neck's worth to do otherwise. Señor Juan López told me as much. And so... come along, Miller Lucas." And he turned towards the door.

"Well, anything stranger...!" said the Miller in a low voice.

"Very strange!" answered Mistress Frasquita.

"There's something... I can see..." Miller Lucas went on, murmuring so low that Tony could not hear.

"Would you like me to go to the City," whispered his wife, "and let the Corregidor know what's happening?"

"No!" replied Miller Lucas aloud. "No! Not that."

"Then what would you like me to do?" said the Miller's wife, ready for anything.

"I'd like you to look at me," answered the ex-soldier.

The couple gazed at one another in silence and drew such satisfaction from the tranquillity, the resolution, and

67

the energy that each poured into the other's soul that they had to grasp each other by the shoulders and laugh.

This done, Miller Lucas lighted another lamp and went off to the stable, calling slily to Tony on the way:

"Come on, man! Come and help me if you'll be so obliging."

Tony followed him, humming a tune through his teeth.

A few minutes later Miller Lucas left the Mill mounted on a fine jenny and followed by the Bailiff.

The farewell of husband and wife was no more than as follows:

"Lock up the house," said Miller Lucas.

"Wrap yourself up, it's cold," said Mistress Frasquita, locking up with bolt, bar, and key.

That was all. No more goodbyes, no more kisses, no more embraces, no more glances.

Why?

XVI. A BIRD OF EVIL OMEN

FOR OUR PART, let us follow Miller Lucas.

They had already covered a quarter of a league without a word, the Miller mounted on his she-ass and the Bailiff driving her from behind with his staff of office, when they observed in front of them, at the top of a rise in the road, an enormous bird which was coming towards them.

The thing stood out sharply against the moonlit sky, depicted upon it with such precision that the Miller exclaimed at once: "Tony, that is Weasel, with his three-cornered hat and his long spindle-shanks."

But before Tony could reply, the shape, anxious doubtless to avoid that encounter, had left the road and set off at a run across country with the speed of a real weasel.

Then Tony replied. "I see no one," he said, in the most natural way in the world.

Miller Lucas swallowed his words. "Neither do I," he answered. And the suspicion which had already occurred to him at the Mill began to take on body and consistency in the distrustful soul of the hunchback.

"This journey of mine," he said to himself, "is a plot of the Corregidor's. What I heard yesterday afternoon from the top of the arbor shows well enough that this old fool from Madrid can't wait any longer. Without a doubt, he's going back to the Mill tonight, and so he has begun by

clearing me out of the way. But what does it matter? Frasquita is Frasquita! Even if they set the house on fire she won't open the door. I'd go further! Even if she did open it, even if the Corregidor managed by some trick to get at my dear girl, the old rogue would soon come out again with his tail between his legs. Frasquita is Frasquita! Still," he added after a moment, "it will be as well for me to get back home tonight as soon as I possibly can."

Hereupon Miller Lucas and the Bailiff reached the Village and made their way to the house of the Mayor.

XVII. A RUSTIC MAYOR

SEÑOR Juan López, who, as man and Mayor, was tyranny, ferocity, and pride personified when dealing with his inferiors, condescended none the less at that time of day, after having despatched his official duties and those of his farm and having given his wife her daily beating, to drink a jug of wine in company with the Secretary and the Sacristan, an operation which was about half completed tonight when the Miller appeared before him.

"Hollo! Miller Lucas," he said, and he scratched his head so as to set his bump of mendacity working. "How are you? Now, Mr. Secretary, a glass of wine for Miller Lucas! And Mistress Frasquita? As fine as ever, I suppose? It's a long time since I've seen her. Ah, man; milling's a fine job nowadays. Rye bread nowadays is as good as the best white. Well, come, sit you down and rest. God be thanked, we're in no hurry."

"Devil a bit, as far as I'm concerned," answered Miller Lucas, who till now had not opened his mouth, but whose suspicions were growing stronger every moment at the friendly reception he was receiving after so formidable and pressing a summons.

"Well then, Miller Lucas," continued the Mayor, "as you're in no great hurry, you'll sleep the night here and early tomorrow we'll despatch our little business."

"Good!" replied Miller Lucas with an irony and dissimulation which were more than a match for the diplomacy of Señor Juan López. "As the thing is not urgent, I don't mind spending the night away from home."

"Neither urgent nor involving any risk for you," added

the Mayor, tricked by the man he thought he himself was tricking. "You can set your mind at rest about that. Here, Tony, hand over that bushel, so that Miller Lucas can sit down."

"More drinks then," cried Miller Lucas, seating himself.

"Help yourself," replied the Mayor, handing him the full glass.

"After you, Sir! After you!"

"Well, here's your very good health," said Señor Juan López, half emptying the glass.

"The same to you, Mr. Mayor!" replied Miller Lucas, draining the second half.

"Hi! Manuela!" called the Mayor. "Tell your mistress that Miller Lucas is staying the night here. Tell her to put him a bolster in the granary."

"No! No! Nothing of the kind. I shall sleep like a king in the straw-loft."

"But we have plenty of bolsters."

"I'm sure you have! But why should you trouble the family? I have my cloak."

"Well, as you like, Sir. Manuela! Tell your mistress not to trouble about the bolster."

"I've only one favor to ask," continued Miller Lucas, yawning atrociously, "and that is that I may go to bed at once. Last night I had a lot of stuff to grind and I haven't had a wink of sleep yet."

"By all means!" replied the Mayor, majestically. "Retire when you feel inclined."

"I think it's time for us to retire as well," said the Sacristan, gazing into the jug to gauge how much wine was left. "It must be ten already, or very near it."

"A quarter to ten," announced the Secretary after sharing among the glasses the rest of the night's allowance of wine.

"Well, to bed, gentlemen," said the host, swallowing his share.

"Good night, Sirs!" added the Miller, drinking his.

"Wait till we get you a light! Tony, take Miller Lucas to the straw-loft."

"This way, Miller Lucas," said Tony, taking the jug with him in case there were a few drops left.

"We meet tomorrow, if God wills," said the Sacristan, finishing the last drop out of each glass. And off he went, staggering as he went and gaily singing the *De Profundis*.

*   *   *   *

"Well, Sir," said the Mayor to the Secretary when they were alone, "Miller Lucas has suspected nothing. We can safely go to bed and…good luck to the Corregidor."

XVIII. IN WHICH IT IS SEEN THAT MILLER LUCAS WAS A VERY LIGHT SLEEPER

FIVE minutes later, a man dropped from the window of the Mayor's straw-loft, a window which gave on a yard and was hardly twelve feet from the ground. In the yard was a shed covering a row of mangers to which were tied six or eight horses, mules and donkeys, all of them mares. The stallions were stabled apart in a place near by.

The man untied a jenny, which was in fact already saddled, and went off, leading her by the bridle, towards the gate of the yard. He undid the bar and loosed the bolt which secured it, opened it cautiously, and found himself in the open country.

Once there, he mounted the jenny, drove his heels into her, and was off like an arrow in the direction of the City, not however by the ordinary cart-way, but over field and dale, as one who keeps clear of some untoward meeting.

It was Miller Lucas making for his Mill.

XIX. *VOCES CLAMANTES*
IN DESERTO

"THAT'S the way we treat Mayors where I come from!" said the Miller to himself as he cantered along. "Tomorrow morning I shall go and see my Lord the Bishop, by way of precaution, and tell him all that has happened tonight. Sending for me with such hurry and secrecy at that time of night! Telling me to come alone! Talking to me of the Service of the King, false money, witches, spooks! And all to hand me a couple of glasses of wine and send me to bed! The thing's as clear as clear can be! Weasel brought those instructions to the Village from the Corregidor, and now the Corregidor will be setting his springes for my wife. Who knows if I shall not find him knocking at the door of the Mill? Who knows if I shall not find him inside already? Who knows? But what am I saying? Suspect my good girl? Oh, that's an offence against God! It's impossible that she...! It's impossible that my Frasquita...! It's impossible...! What am I talking about? Is there anything in the world impossible? Didn't she marry me, beautiful as she is, and me so ugly?" And at the thought of that the poor hunchback began to weep.

Then he reined in his jenny so as to calm himself a little, wiped his tears, sighed deeply, drew out his pouch and rolled himself a cigarette, took his flint, tinder, and steel, and after striking once or twice, succeeded in getting a light.

At that moment he heard a sound of footsteps on the road, which was about three hundred yards away from where he had stopped.

"I'm a silly fool," he said. "Suppose they're after me already! I shall have given myself away by striking that light."

So saying, he put out the light, dismounted, and took cover behind the jenny.

But the jenny understood the situation differently and let out a bray of satisfaction.

"Confound the beast!" exclaimed Miller Lucas, trying to shut her mouth with his hands.

Just then another bray rang out from the road, by way of gallant reply.

"We're done for!" thought the Miller to himself. "The song's right:

> Woes are fiftyfold increased
> For the man that trusts a beast."

And reflecting thus, he mounted again, clapped heels to his jenny and set off headlong in the direction opposite to that of the answering bray.

And the strange thing was that the person who rode the other ass must have taken fright at Miller Lucas just as

Miller Lucas had taken fright at him. I say so because he too left the road, doubtless suspecting that it was a Bailiff or some rascal in the pay of Don Eugenio, and went off at a gallop across the fields at the other side of the road.

The Miller, meanwhile, thus continued his reflections:

"What a night! What a world! What a life I've led during the last hour! Bailiffs turned into pimps! Mayors plotting against my honor, donkeys braying when they ought not; and here, in my breast, a wretched heart which has dared to suspect the noblest wife that God ever created! Oh! My God, my God! Grant that I may come quickly home and find my Frasquita safe."

Miller Lucas went on his way over field and thicket, until at last, about eleven of the night, he came without further adventure to the great door of the Mill.

Damnation! The door of the Mill was open!

IT WAS OPEN! Yet when he set out from home he had heard his wife fasten it with bolt, bar, and key.

Consequently, none but his wife herself could have opened it.

But how? When? Why? Because of a trick? In obedience to an order? Or of her own free will and resolve, in virtue of a previous understanding with the Corregidor?

What was he going to see? What was he going to discover? What awaited him in his home? Could Frasquita have flown? Had they kidnapped her? Was she dead? Or was she in the arms of his rival?

"The Corregidor reckoned that I could not get back all night," said Miller Lucas to himself gloomily. "The Mayor of the Village must have had orders to put me under lock and key rather than let me return. Did Frasquita know all that? Was she in the plot? Or has she been the victim of a trick, of violence, of infamy?"

Over these cruel reflections the unlucky fellow spent no more time than it took him to cross the little court of the arbor.

The house door too was open. The first room (as in all country dwellings) was the kitchen.

In the kitchen there was nobody.

None the less, an enormous fire was blazing in the fire-

place, though there was no fire when he went out nor did they ever light one there until well on in December.

Lastly, from one of the hooks of the rack hung a lighted lamp.

What could it all mean? How reconcile these signs of wakefulness and company with the deathly silence that reigned throughout the house?

What had become of his wife?

Then, and then only, Miller Lucas caught sight of certain clothes hung over the backs of two or three chairs set round the fire.

On those clothes he fixed his eyes and let out a growl so deep that it stuck in his throat, and changed into a dumb and suffocating sob.

The wretched man felt himself choking and raised his hands to his neck while, livid, convulsed, his eyes starting out of his head, he stared at that clothing with the horror of a criminal at the point of death when they offer him the sack of execution.

For what he saw before him was the scarlet cape, the three-cornered hat, the dove-colored coat and waistcoat, the black silk breeches, the white stockings, the buckled shoes, down to the very stick, sword and gloves of the execrable Corregidor. What he saw before him was the death-sack of his shame, the shroud of his murdered honor, the extinction of his happiness.

The terrible blunderbuss stood in the same corner where, two hours before, his wife had left it. Miller Lucas sprang on it like a tiger and seized it in his hands. He tried the barrel with the ramrod and found that it was loaded. He examined the flint and saw that it was in place. Then he turned to the staircase which led to the room in which for so many years he had slept with Mistress Frasquita, and murmured dully:

"They are there!"

He took one step in that direction; but next moment he paused to look round him and see if anyone was watching.

"Nobody!" he said to himself. "Only God, and He... has willed this!"

Having thus confirmed the sentence, he was just going to take another step when his wandering gaze detected a folded paper lying on the table.

To see it, to hurl himself upon it, to hold it in his clutch, was the work of a second.

That paper was the nomination of Mistress Frasquita's nephew, signed by Don Eugenio de Zúñiga y Ponce de León!

"This," thought Miller Lucas, "is the price. She has sold herself," and he crammed the paper into his mouth to stifle his cries and give nourishment to his fury. "I always suspected that she loved her family more than me. Ah! We never had children! That's what caused it all."

And the unhappy man was on the point of bursting into tears again. But at that moment fury came upon him once more and with a terrible gesture rather than by word of mouth he exclaimed:

"Upstairs! Upstairs!"

And he began to climb the stairs like a beast, one hand on the floor, the other grasping the blunderbuss, with the infamous paper between his teeth.

In corroboration of his suspicions, on arriving at the bedroom door, which was locked, he saw a light through the keyhole and at the joins in the woodwork.

"Here they are!" he muttered again. And he stood for a moment as if to drain this new cup of bitterness.

Not a sound came from within.

"Suppose there's no one there," whispered the timid voice of hope. But at that very instant the unhappy man heard someone cough in the room.

It was the asthmatical cough of the Corregidor.

Not a doubt remained; not a plank of salvation in his immense shipwreck!

In the darkness the Miller smiled horribly. How can darkness be dark before such flashes of the soul? What are all the fires of torture compared with that which sometimes burns in the heart of man?

None the less, no sooner had he heard his enemy's cough, than Miller Lucas (for such was his soul, as we have already said elsewhere) began to grow calm. The reality hurt him less than the suspicion. As he himself had said that evening to Mistress Frasquita, from the moment in which he had lost the one faith which was the life of his soul, he began to change into a new man.

Like the Moor of Venice (with whom we have already compared him in describing his character), disillusionment slew all his love at a single blow, transforming at once the nature of his spirit and forcing him to look upon the world as a strange land in which he had just arrived. The one difference was that by temperament Miller Lucas was less tragic, less austere, and more of an egoist than the insensate sacrificer of Desdemona.

Strange but true of such situations—doubt, or rather

hope (which in this case is the same) came back again and subdued him for a moment!

"What if I were mistaken!" he thought. "What if the cough were Frasquita's!"

In the agony of his mischance he forgot that he had seen the clothes of the Corregidor round the kitchen fire, that he had found the door of the Mill open, that he had read the proof of his disgrace.

He stooped and looked through the keyhole, trembling with doubt and anguish.

His glance could only discover a little triangle of bed, up beside the head. But precisely in that little triangle appeared one end of the pillows, and on the pillows the head of the Corregidor.

Once more a diabolical laugh distorted the face of the Miller. It was almost as if he were happy once again.

"Now I know the truth," he murmured, straightening himself calmly. "Let me think."

And he went downstairs again with the same precautions with which he had gone up.

"It's a ticklish subject. I must reflect. I have plenty of time for *everything*," he thought as he descended.

When he had reached the kitchen he sat down in the middle of the room and covered his face with his hands.

So he remained for a long while, until he was roused from his meditation by a light blow on one foot. It was

the blunderbuss which had slipped from his knees and had chosen that way of attracting his attention.

"No! I tell you, no!" murmured Miller Lucas, face to face with the weapon. "You are not what I want. Everyone would pity *them*, and they'd hang *me*. We are dealing with a Corregidor, and in Spain it is still an unforgivable sin to kill a Corregidor. They would say that I killed him from unfounded jealousy and then undressed him and put him in my bed. They would say too, that I killed my wife simply on suspicion . . . and they'd hang me. Most certainly they'd hang me! Besides, I should have shown myself very small-souled, very little-witted if in the ending of my life I had earned nothing but pity. Everyone would laugh at me. They would say that my ill-luck was very natural, when I was a hunchback and Frasquita so beautiful. No! Nothing of the sort! What I want is to revenge myself, and, after that, to triumph, scorn, laugh, laugh hugely, laugh at everybody, so that no one will ever be able to make fun of this hump which I have made almost enviable, and which would look so grotesque on a gallows."

So reasoned Miller Lucas, without perhaps taking account of it word by word; and in virtue of some such reasoning he put back the weapon in its place and began to pace to and fro with his hands behind him and his head bowed, as if seeking for his revenge on the ground, in the earth, in all that is base in life, in some ridiculous and ig-

nominious joke against his wife and the Corregidor, far from seeking that same revenge in the law, in a challenge, in forgiveness, or in Heaven, as any other man of a condition less rebellious against all the dictates of human nature, society, or his own feelings, would have done in his place.

Suddenly his gaze came to rest on the clothes of the Corregidor. He stood still.

And then, little by little, there spread over his face an indefinable look of joy, of glee, of triumph, until at last he burst out laughing, hugely, in great guffaws, but without making a sound (for fear they should hear him upstairs), clutching his hands to his sides to stop himself bursting, the whole man shuddering like an epileptic, forced at last to drop into a chair until that convulsion of sarcastic merriment had left him. It was the laugh of Mephistopheles himself.

The moment he was calm again, he set about stripping himself with feverish haste, laid all his clothes on the chairs formerly occupied by those of the Corregidor, dressed himself in the latter, from the buckled shoes to the three-cornered hat; girt on the sword; wrapped himself up in the scarlet cape; snatched up the stick and the gloves, and left the mill and set off for the City, waddling just as Don Eugenio de Zúñiga waddled, and now and then muttering to himself this phrase, which very aptly summed the thought that possessed him:

"Well, the Corregidor's Lady is a fine woman too!"

XXI. ON GUARD, MY LORD!

AND NOW let us leave Miller Lucas and take a look at what had happened at the Mill from the time that we left Mistress Frasquita alone there until her husband returned to make these astounding discoveries.

An hour had gone by since Miller Lucas went off with Tony, when his distressed wife, who had resolved not to go to bed until her husband returned and now sat knitting in her bedroom which was on the upper floor, heard pitiful cries outside the house in the direction of the millrace, which was close to that part of the building.

"Help! I'm drowning! Frasquita! Frasquita!" It was a man's voice and its accent was the melancholy accent of despair.

"Can it be Lucas?" she thought, filled with a terror that we hardly need describe.

In the bedroom was a little door, of which Weasel has told us already, which gave on the upper part of the millrace. Without a moment's hesitation, Mistress Frasquita opened it, although she had not recognized the voice that called for help, and to her amazement found herself face to face with the Corregidor who at that very moment was emerging, his clothes streaming with water, from the headlong rush of the channel.

"God forgive me! God forgive me!" babbled the infamous old man. "I thought I was drowning!"

"Why! It's your Honor! What's the meaning of this? How dare you? What do you want to come here for at this time of day?" cried the Miller's wife, more indignant than afraid, though mechanically she retreated.

"Hush! Hush, woman!" stammered the Corregidor, slipping into the room behind her. "I will tell you all. I was within an ace of drowning. The water was on the point of sweeping me away like a feather. Look, look at the state I'm in!"

"Out you go from here," replied Mistress Frasquita with growing vehemence. "You need explain nothing! I understand it all too well! What do I care whether you drown or not? Did I ask you to come? Ah, the infamy of it! That's why you sent for my husband!"

"Woman, listen...!"

"I won't listen! Off you go at once, Sir! Off you go, or I won't answer for your life!"

"What are you saying?"

"I'm saying what I mean. My husband's not at home, but I'm quite capable of protecting our home myself. Off you go, to where you come from, unless you want me to take you and throw you back into the water!"

"My dear, my dear, don't shout so! I'm not deaf!" exclaimed the old rake. "If I'm here, it's for a good reason. I have come to free Miller Lucas, whom a Village Mayor has arrested by mistake. But, first of all, you must dry these clothes for me. I'm soaked to the skin."

94

"Off you go, I tell you."

"Be quiet, foolish creature! What do you know about it? Look, I've brought you your nephew's nomination. Light the lamp and we'll talk about it. And while these clothes are drying, I'll get into this bed here."

"Ah! So you confess you've come to see *me?* You confess that's why you sent and had Lucas arrested? So you were bringing the nomination and all? Saints of Heaven! What sort of an idea has this old figure of fun got of me?"

"Frasquita! I am the Corregidor!"

"If you were the King himself, what has it got to do with *me?* I'm the wife of my husband, and the mistress of my house! Do you think I'm frightened of Corregidors? I'll go to Madrid, I'd go to the world's end, for justice against the insolent old rogue who drags his authority in the mud like this. And, what's more, tomorrow morning I'll put on my mantilla and go and see her Ladyship!"

"You'll do nothing of the sort!" replied the Corregidor, losing patience, or changing his tactics. "You'll do nothing of the sort; because, if I see that you're not going to listen to reason, I'll put a bullet through you."

"A bullet?" exclaimed Mistress Frasquita in a low voice.

"Yes, a bullet! And it will do me no damage, either. As it happens, I've left word in the City that I was coming out tonight after certain miscreants. And so don't be silly, but love me…as I adore you!"

"A bullet, Sir?" repeated the Miller's wife, putting her arms behind her and throwing her body forward as if to spring upon her opponent.

"If you give me trouble, I shall shoot you, and then I shall be free of your threats and your beauty," answered the terrified Corregidor, taking out a pair of pocket-pistols.

"Pistols too! And my nephew's nomination in the other pocket!" said Mistress Frasquita, nodding her head up and down. "Then, Sir, I have no choice. Wait a moment, I'm going to light the light."

So saying, she ran to the stairs and in three leaps was down them.

The Corregidor snatched up the light and went after her, fearing she would escape; but he had to take the stairs much more slowly, with the result that, when he reached the kitchen, he ran into Frasquita who was already coming back in search of him.

"So, you were saying, you would put a bullet through me?" cried the indomitable woman, taking a pace backwards. "Then, on guard, my Lord! I'm ready for you!"

So saying, she raised to her cheek the formidable blunderbuss which plays so important a part in this history.

"Stop, wretched creature! What are you about?" shouted the Corregidor, half dead with fright. "My bullet was a joke. Look, the pistols are unloaded. On the other hand it's true about the nomination. Here it is! Take it! I give it you! It's yours...for nothing...free, gratis, and for nothing!"

He placed it, trembling, upon the table.

"Good!" replied Frasquita. "I'll light the fire with it to-morrow when I cook my husband's breakfast. I wouldn't take salvation itself from you now; and if sometime my nephew comes from Estella, it will be to stamp his foot on the foul hand that wrote his name on that filthy paper. There now! So off you go out of my house! Quick, now: quick! I'm beginning to lose my temper!"

The Corregidor made no reply to this outburst. He had grown livid, almost blue; his eyes were distorted, his whole body was shaken by a tremor like ague. Then his teeth began to chatter and he fell to the ground in the grip of a horrible convulsion.

The shock of the mill-race, the drenched state of his clothing, the violent scene in the bedroom, his terror of the blunderbuss which Frasquita held to his head, had sapped the strength of the feeble old man.

"I'm dying!" he babbled. "Call Weasel! Call Weasel! he's there in the gully. I must not die in this house!" He could say no more. He closed his eyes and lay as if dead.

"And if he dies, as he says," broke out Mistress Frasquita, "that would be the worst job of all. What am I doing with this man in my house? What will they say about me, if he dies? What will Lucas say? How can I clear myself, when it was I myself who opened the door? Oh, no! I can't stay here with him. I must go and find my husband; rather than folk should think ill of me I'll disgrace the lot of them."

Having so resolved, she put by the blunderbuss, ran to the yard, took the remaining jenny, saddled it anyhow, mounted it at a bound, despite her goodly size, and made for the gully.

"Weasel! Weasel!" she shouted, as she approached the spot.

"Here!" replied the Bailiff, appearing behind a fence. "Is it you, Mistress Frasquita?"

"Yes, it's me! Go to the Mill and look after your master, who's at death's door!"

"What? You're joking."

"It's the plain truth, Weasel!"

"And you, my good soul; where are you off to at this time of night?"

"Me! Mind your own business! I'm going ... to the City to fetch a doctor," answered Mistress Frasquita with a kick to the donkey and another to Weasel, and off she went. But she took, not the road to the City as she had just said, but the one to the neighboring Village.

Weasel did not notice this last circumstance, for he was striding already on his long shanks towards the Mill, his mind busy with some such thoughts as these:

"Going for the doctor! What else could the woman do? But *he's* a poor sort of man! A nice time to be ill! Well, God gives all the plums to them that can't eat them!"

XXII. WEASEL EXCELS HIMSELF

WHEN WEASEL reached the Mill, the Corregidor was beginning to come around, and was trying to get up off the floor. On the floor too, just beside him, stood the lighted lamp which his Honor had brought down from the bedroom.

"Has it gone?" was Don Eugenio's first remark.

"Has what gone?"

"The devil, I mean the Miller-woman!"

"Yes, my Lord, she's gone. And not in the best of tempers, I think!"

"Ah, Weasel! I'm dying!"

"But what's the matter with your Honor? Man alive...!"

"I fell into the mill-race and I'm sopped to the skin. I'm perished to the very bones!"

"Well, I never! And it's come to this!"

"Weasel, mind what you say!"

"I'm saying nothing, my Lord!"

"Very well! Help me out of this!"

"This very minute! Your Honor'll see, I'll put everything right at once."

No sooner said than done. The Bailiff took the lamp in one hand and with the other tucked the Corregidor under his arm and carried him up to the bedroom, stripped him stark naked, put him to bed, ran to the shed, snatched up an armful of wood, ran back to the kitchen, made a great fire, took down all his master's clothes, hung them on the backs of two or three chairs, lighted a stable lamp, hung it on the rack, and went up to the bedroom again.

"How are we now?" he asked Don Eugenio, holding the lamp high to get a better view of his face.

"Admirable! I shall be sweating soon! Tomorrow, Weasel, you'll hang for this!"

"But why, my Lord!"

"And you dare to ask why? Do you think, when I followed your precious plan, that I expected to end up alone in this bed, after receiving the sacrament of baptism for the second time? Yes, you shall hang tomorrow."

"But tell me something about it. Mistress Frasquita...?"

"Mistress Frasquita tried to murder me. That's all I've got out of your advice. Tomorrow morning, I tell you, you shall hang."

"It won't be as bad as that, my Lord!" answered the Bailiff.

"Why not, you saucy fellow? Because you've got me here on my back?"

"No, my Lord! Because Mistress Frasquita can't have been quite so cruel as you say, when she's gone to the City to fetch a doctor for you!"

"Good God! Are you sure she's gone to the City?" cried Don Eugenio, more terrified than ever.

"She told me so, anyhow!"

"Run, run, Weasel! Oh, I'm done for, hopelessly done for! Do you know why Mistress Frasquita has gone to the City? To tell the whole business to my wife! To tell her that I'm here! My God, my God! I never thought of that. I thought she had gone to the Village to find her husband; and as I've got him safe and snug she was free to go there, for all I cared. But if she's gone to the City...! Run, Weasel, run...you're a good runner...and save me from perdition! Stop that wild Miller-woman from getting into my house!"

"And if I do, your Honor'll let me off the hanging?" asked the Bailiff ironically.

"Instead of a hanging, I'll give you a good pair of boots which are too big for me. I'll give you anything you like."

"Then I'll be off. Let your Honor sleep in peace. In half an hour I'll be back and Frasquita will be in jail. I can be quicker than a donkey when I like."

So saying, Weasel disappeared down the stairs.

It so fell out that precisely when the Bailiff was away, the Miller came back to his Mill and saw signs and wonders through the keyhole.

So let us leave the Corregidor sweating in a strange bed and Weasel running to the City (whither Miller Lucas with the three-cornered hat and the scarlet cloak was to follow hard on his heels), and, ourselves too becoming runners, let us fly towards the Village in the train of the valiant Mistress Frasquita.

XXIII. AGAIN THE DESERT &
THE AFOREMENTIONED VOICES

THE ONLY adventure which befell the Miller's wife on her journey from the Mill to the hamlet was to be somewhat startled at observing someone striking a light in the middle of a field.

"Suppose it's some ruffian of the Corregidor's! I shall be stopped," she thought to herself.

At that moment there came from the same direction a loud bray.

"Donkeys loose at this time of the night!" thought Mistress Frasquita, "when there's no orchard or farm hereabouts! God bless us if ghosts aren't up to their games tonight. Surely my husband's jenny couldn't be...! Nay, what would Lucas be doing at midnight, halting, away off the road? No! No! Without doubt, it's a spy!"

The jenny which Mistress Frasquita was riding thought fit, at that moment, to bray too.

"Be quiet, you she-devil!" said the Miller's wife, sticking a two-inch pin into her withers.

And, fearing some untoward encounter, she too turned her beast off the road and trotted away across the fields at the other side.

Without further mischance she reached the gates of the Village at eleven of the night or thereabouts.

XXIV. A MONARCH OF THAT TIME

THE MAYOR was sleeping off the effects of his evening's potations, his back burned to the back of his wife (thus assuming with her the form of the two-headed Austrian Eagle, as the immortal Quevedo has remarked), when Tony knocked at the door of the nuptial chamber and informed Señor Juan López that "Mistress Frasquita from the Mill" wished to speak with him.

It is not for us to record all the snarling and swearing which accompanied the waking and dressing of the Mayor, and so we transport ourselves to the moment when he appeared before the Miller's wife, stretching himself like a gymnast exercising his muscles, and exclaiming in the middle of an endless yawn:

"How d'you do, Mistress Frasquita! What brings you here? Didn't Tony tell you that you must stay at the Mill? Is this the way you obey the Authorities?"

"I must see Lucas!" answered the Miller's wife. "I must see him at once! Please tell them to let him know that his wife is here!"

"*I must! I must!* You forget, Ma'am, that you're talking to the King!"

"Leave Kings alone, Señor Juan; I'm in no mood for jokes! You know well enough what's happened to me! You know well enough why you've arrested my husband!"

"I know nothing, Mistress Frasquita. And as for your husband, he's not been arrested: he's sleeping peacefully in this house, treated as well as I always treat visitors. Here, Tony! Go to the straw-loft and tell Miller Lucas to get up and come here at once. Well now, Mistress Frasquita, tell me what's happened. Were you afraid to sleep alone?"

"Think shame of yourself, Señor Juan. You know well enough that it's no good your trying to deceive me. What's happened is soon told. You and the Corregidor have done your best to ruin me, but you've made a mess of it. Here I am without a stain on my character, and the Corregidor is at the Mill, dying."

"The Corregidor dying!" exclaimed his underling. "Madam, do you know what you're saying?"

"Yes, it's the truth. He fell into the mill-race and nearly drowned himself, and now he's got pneumonia or Heaven knows what.... That's her Ladyship's concern. I've come to find my husband, and even when I've found him it won't prevent me starting for Madrid tomorrow to inform the King..."

"The devil! The devil!" murmured Señor Juan López. "Here, Manuela! Girl! Go and saddle me the little mule. Mistress Frasquita, I'm off to the Mill and woe betide you if you've done any harm to the Corregidor!"

At that moment Tony came in, more dead than alive.

"Mr. Mayor! Mr. Mayor!" he exclaimed. "Miller Lucas

is not in the straw-loft. And his jenny is not in the stables either, and the yard door is open. Your bird's flown!"

"What are you talking about?"cried Señor Juan López.

"Holy Virgin! Then what will be happening at home!" exclaimed Mistress Frasquita. "Come, let us hurry, Mr. Mayor; we must lose no time. My husband will murder the Corregidor when he finds him there at this time of night."

"Then you think Miller Lucas is at the Mill?"

"Well, haven't I good reason to? I'll say more…On my way here I passed him without knowing him. Without a doubt it was he who was striking a light in the middle of a field. Good Lord! To think that animals have more sense than human souls! For I may tell you, Señor Juan, that undoubtedly our two donkeys recognized each another and wished each other good evening, while Lucas and I did neither. Far from it; we ran for our lives, each thinking the other was a spy."

"Your Lucas will land himself in a pretty pickle," replied the Mayor. "Come, let us be off, and we'll see what's to be done with the lot of you. You can't play tricks with me. I'm the King; and not a King like the one we have now in Madrid, or out at El Prado, but like the one they had in Seville, that they called Don Pedro the Cruel. Here, Manuela! Bring me my stick, and tell your Mistress that I'm going out."

The servant obeyed (she was a better girl, certainly, than the Mayor's wife and the reputation of his house deserved), and, as Señor Juan López's little mule was ready-saddled, Mistress Frasquita and he set off for the Mill, followed by the indispensable Tony.

XXV.

WEASEL'S STAR

WE OURSELVES, who enjoy the privilege of travelling faster than anyone else, will precede them.

Weasel had already got back to the Mill, after having ransacked every street in the City for Mistress Frasquita.

The wily Bailiff had looked in, on his way, at Headquarters, where he found everything perfectly quiet. The doors were still open as in daytime, as is the custom when the Authority is out in the town exercising its sacred functions. Other Bailiffs and petty officers were dozing on the landing of the staircase and in the hall, peacefully awaiting their master; but when they heard Weasel arrive, two or three of them stretched themselves and asked their immediate senior and chief:

"Is the Master coming?"

"Not he! Don't disturb yourselves! I looked in to see if anything had happened…"

"Nothing!"

"And her Ladyship?"

"Her Ladyship has retired to her own apartments."

"Did no woman come, a short time ago?"

"No one has been here all night."

"Then don't let anyone in, whoever he is and whatever he says. Arrest him instead. If the morning star itself comes to ask after the Master and her Ladyship, arrest it and put it in the jail."

"Then you're after rare birds tonight?" asked one of the officers.

"Big-game hunting!" added another.

"Yes, the biggest!" answered Weasel solemnly. "You can imagine it's something rather delicate when the Corregidor and I are doing the hunting ourselves. Well, goodbye, boys; and mind, keep a sharp eye on things!"

"Good luck to you, Señor Bastian!" answered all, saluting Weasel.

"My star's on the wane!" he murmured as he went out of Headquarters. "Even the women fool me! The Miller's wife went to the Village to seek her husband instead of coming to the City. Poor old Weasel! What's become of your scent?"

Thus ruminating he took the turn to the Mill.

The Bailiff's doubts of his ancient powers were not ill-founded, for he failed to scent a man who at that moment was hiding behind some willows, not far from the gully, and who muttered in his sleeve, or rather in his scarlet cloak:

"Look out, my boy! Here comes Weasel! He mustn't catch me here!"

It was Miller Lucas, dressed as the Corregidor, who was on his way to the City, every now and then repeating his diabolical phrase:

"Well, her Ladyship's a fine woman too!"

Weasel went by without seeing him and the false Corregidor left his hiding-place and made his way into the town.

Shortly afterwards, the Bailiff reached the Mill, as we have already recorded.

XXVI. REACTION

THE CORREGIDOR was still in bed, exactly as Miller Lucas had just seen him through the keyhole.

"I'm sweating finely, Weasel! I've saved myself from a dangerous illness!" he exclaimed as the Bailiff entered the room. "What about Mistress Frasquita? Did you come across her? Is she with you? Has she seen my Lady?"

"The Miller's wife, my Lord," answered Weasel in agonized tones, "has fooled me properly. She didn't go to the City; she went to the Village... to find her husband. Let your Honor forgive my stupidity!"

"Better! Far better!" cried the old man of Madrid, his eyes sparkling with iniquity. "Then all's well again! Before dawn the pair of them will be on their way to the jail of the Inquisition, and there they can rot. They'll find no one there to whom they can tell tonight's adventures. Bring me my clothes, Weasel; they must be dry by now! Bring them up and help me to dress! The lover is going to change into the Corregidor!"

Weasel went down to the kitchen for the clothes.

MEANWHILE, Mistress Frasquita, Señor Juan López and Tony advanced upon the Mill, which they reached a few minutes later.

"I'll go first!" exclaimed the Village Mayor. "I'm not 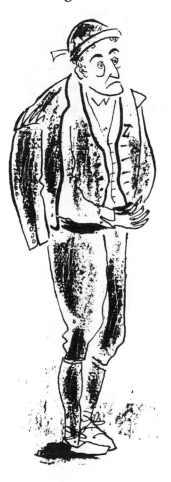 the Authority for nothing! Follow me, Tony; and you, Mistress Frasquita, wait at the door till I call you."

Then Señor Juan López went in under the vine-arbor, where by the light of the moon he saw a man, almost hunchbacked, dressed like the Miller, in a waistcoat and breeches of grey cloth, black sash, blue stockings, a plush Murcian cap, and a cape on his shoulder.

"It's him!" cried the Mayor. "In the King's name! Give yourself up, Miller Lucas!"

The figure in the cap tried to get back into the Mill.

"Surrender!" shouted Tony in turn, leaping on the man, seizing him by the neck, thrusting a knee into his back, and sending him rolling on the ground.

At the same moment another kind of beast sprang upon Tony, and, clutching him by the belt, flung him down on the pavement and began to drub him soundly.

It was Mistress Frasquita.

"Villain!" she cried. "Leave my Lucas alone!"

Thereupon another person who had come on the scene, leading a donkey, threw himself resolutely between the two, and tried to rescue Tony.

It was Weasel, who had mistaken the Village Mayor for Don Eugenio de Zúñiga.

"Madam," he shouted to the Miller's wife, "kindly respect my Master!" and he knocked her down on the top of Tony.

Mistress Frasquita, finding herself between two fires, gave Weasel such a backhander in the middle of the stomach that he measured his length on the pavement.

There were now, including Weasel, four people rolling on the ground.

Meanwhile Señor Juan López was preventing the supposed Miller Lucas from getting on to his feet by planting one foot on the small of his back.

"Weasel! Help! In the King's name! I'm the Corregidor!" cried Don Eugenio, who was almost bursting under the pressure of the Mayor's hoof, which was shod with a bull's-hide clog.

"The Corregidor! So it is!" said Señor Juan López, cold with consternation.

"The Corregidor!" repeated everybody.

And soon all four sprawlers were on their feet again.

"To jail with the lot of them!" cried Don Eugenio de Zúñiga. "To the gallows with the whole pack!"

"But, my Lord…!" observed Señor Juan López, falling on his knees, "your Honor must forgive me for ill-treating you! How was I to know your Honor in common clothes like these?"

"Ruffian!" replied the Corregidor. "I had to put something on, hadn't I? Don't you know that they've stolen mine? Don't you know that a gang of thieves, sent by Miller Lucas…"

"You lie!" cried the Miller's wife.

"Listen to me, Mistress Frasquita!" said Weasel, calling her aside—"By your leave, my Lord Corregidor and company!—If you don't put this right, Ma'am, they'll hang the lot of us, beginning with your Lucas."

"But what's happening?" asked Mistress Frasquita.

"Miller Lucas is, at this very moment, on his way to the City disguised as the Corregidor… and God alone knows if he hasn't got into her Ladyship's very bedroom by this time."

And the Bailiff told her in four words what we know already.

"Holy Jesus!" cried the Miller's wife. "Then my husband believes I'm disgraced! He's gone to the City to have his revenge! Come, let us be off at once to the City and prove to Lucas that I'm innocent!"

"To the City at once! We'll stop this fellow seeing my wife and telling her all this stuff and nonsense that he's got into his head!" said the Corregidor, making for one of the donkeys. "Give me a leg up, Mr. Mayor!"

"Yes, to the City!" added Weasel. "And Heaven grant, Sir, that Miller Lucas, in your clothes, has contented himself with talking to her Ladyship!"

"Miserable creature, what are you talking about?" burst out Don Eugenio de Zúñiga. "Do you imagine the villain is capable...?"

"He's capable of everything!" answered Mistress Frasquita.

XXVIII. HALF-PAST TWELVE
AND A FINE NIGHT!

THUS was the watch crying through the streets of the City when the Miller's wife, the Corregidor, each on one of the Mill donkeys, Señor Juan López on his mule, and the two Bailiffs on foot, came to the door of Headquarters.

The door was shut. For Governors and Governed alike, it seemed, everything was over for that day.

"That looks bad!" thought Weasel. And he beat two or three times on the great knocker.

Time passed, and nobody opened or answered.

Mistress Frasquita's face was yellower than wax.

The Corregidor had already gnawed away all the nails of both hands.

No one spoke a word.

Poom! Poom! Poom! Knocks and knocks again on the door of Headquarters! The Bailiffs and Señor Juan López took turns with the great knocker. And nothing! Nobody replied! Nobody opened! Not a mouse stirred!

Only there came the clear ripple of a fountain from the court within.

And so the minutes ran by, long as eternities.

At last, about one o'clock, a little window opened on the second floor and a woman's voice called:

"Who's there?"

"That's the Wet-Nurse's voice!" muttered Weasel.

"It's I!" answered Don Eugenio de Zúñiga. "Open the door!"

There was a moment's silence.

Then came the Wet-Nurse's voice again. "And who are you?"

"Can't you hear who I am? I'm the Master! The Corregidor!"

There was another pause.

"Off you go, and good night to you!" answered the good woman. "My Master came in an hour ago and went straight to bed. You had best go to bed, too, and sleep off some of that drink you've been filling your stomachs with!"

Again the window was slammed to.

Mistress Frasquita covered her face with her hands.

"Nurse!" thundered the Corregidor, beside himself with rage. "Open the door; don't you hear me? Can't you hear it's me! Do you want me to hang you too?"

The window opened once more.

"Come, let's see! Who are you to be shouting like that?" hazarded the Nurse.

"I'm the Corregidor!"

"Get along with you, you humbug! Aren't I telling you that my Lord the Corregidor came in before twelve, and I saw him with my own eyes lock himself into her Ladyship's apartments? But if you must have your joke, then wait a minute! You'll see!"

At the same moment the door opened suddenly and a whole host of servants and understrappers, armed with

sticks, threw themselves on the party outside, shouting furiously:

"Let's see him! Where's this fellow who says he's the Corregidor? Where is he; the wag, the drunkard?"

And then there broke out in the darkness the Devil's own shindy; nobody knew where he was, and the Corregidor, Weasel, Señor Juan López, and Tony all came in for their share of whacks.

That was the second drubbing that the night's adventure had cost Don Eugenio, to say nothing of the soaking he had given himself in the mill-race.

Mistress Frasquita, who had managed to keep out of the tangle, was, for the first time in her life, weeping bitterly.

"Lucas! Lucas!" she cried. "How could you suspect me! How could you clasp another in your arms! Ah! There's no remedy now for our misfortune!"

"WHAT IS THIS disturbance?" The calm, dignified voice, with its pleasant tone, sounded across the hurly-burly.

All raised their faces and saw that a woman dressed in black stood looking down from the chief balcony of the building.

"Her Ladyship!" said the servants, and they paused in their beating of those human drums.

"My wife!" stammered Don Eugenio.

"Let them come in. The Corregidor says that they are to be admitted," added her Ladyship.

The servants made way and Don Eugenio and his companions entered the porch and began to climb the staircase.

Never did criminal approach the gibbet with step so uncertain and countenance so altered as those of the Corregidor when he mounted the stairs of his own home. None the less, the idea of his dishonor was already beginning to surpass, in his mind's noble egoism, all the misfortunes which he had brought on others and himself, and the absurdities of the situation in which he now found himself.

"Before all," he thought, as he climbed the stair, "I am a Zúñiga and a Ponce de León! And woe betide those who have forgotten it! Woe betide my wife if she has sullied my name!"

XXX. A GREAT LADY

HER LADYSHIP received her spouse and the rustic company in the principal salon.

She was alone, and stood waiting for them, her eyes fastened on the door.

She was a lady of great distinction, still tolerably young, of a calm and severe beauty more suited to the Christian painter than the Classic sculptor, and she was dressed with all the stateliness and sobriety conformable with the taste of the period. Her dress—the short, narrow skirt and the high, puffed sleeves—was of black bombazine; a shawl of blond lace of a yellowish tinge veiled her admirable shoulders, and long mittens of black tulle almost entirely covered her arms, which were white as alabaster. One hand wafted with slow dignity a huge fan, brought from the Philippine Islands; in the other she held a lace handkerchief whose four corners hung down symmetrically with an orderliness to be compared only with that of her attitude and minor movements.

This beautiful woman inspired all who beheld her with reverence and fear, for she had about her something of the queen and much of the abbess. For the rest, the punctiliousness of her dress at such an hour, the gravity of her bearing, and the fact that the salon was brilliantly lighted, showed that her Ladyship had taken some pains to impart to that scene a dramatic solemnity, a touch of ceremony, which contrasted strikingly with the coarse and vulgar character of her husband's adventure.

Finally, let us remark that this Lady was named Doña Mercedes Carrillo de Albornoz y Espinosa de los Monteros, and that she was a daughter, granddaughter, great-granddaughter, great-great-granddaughter, and all the way to twentieth granddaughter of the City, being a descendant of its illustrious Conquistadors. Her family, for reasons of worldly vanity, had persuaded her to marry the wealthy old Corregidor, and she, who would otherwise have been a nun, since her natural vocation drew her to the cloister, had consented to this grievous sacrifice.

At this time she had already borne two children to that gay old dog from Madrid, and it was whispered that there was yet another on the way.

And so let us return to our story.

XXXI. THE PAINS OF RETRIBUTION

"MERCEDES!" exclaimed the Corregidor as he entered the presence of his spouse. "I must be told at once..."

"Ah, Miller Lucas! You here?" her Ladyship interrupted. "Is there anything the matter at the Mill?"

"I'm in no humor for jokes, Ma'am!" replied the Corregidor, wild with rage. "Before entering upon any explanations of my own, I must know how my honor stands..."

"That is not my affair! Did you leave it in my keeping?"

"Yes, Ma'am! In your keeping!" replied Don Eugenio. "Wives are the keepers of their husbands' honor."

"Then, my good Miller Lucas, ask your wife. There she is, listening to us!"

Mistress Frasquita, who had remained at the door of the salon, gave a kind of growl.

"Come in, Mistress, and sit down," added her Ladyship, addressing the Miller's wife with superb dignity; and she herself went over to the sofa.

Mistress Frasquita, noble creature that she was, saw and appreciated from that moment the true greatness of the attitude of that injured, and perhaps doubly injured, wife. And so, rising at once to an equal height, she controlled her natural impulses and preserved a dignified silence. Nor had that silence anything to do with the fact that Mistress Frasquita, secure in her strength and her innocence, was

in no hurry to defend herself. For she was in a hurry, a great hurry, to accuse; though certainly not to accuse her Ladyship. No, it was with Miller Lucas that she wished to settle her account, and Miller Lucas was not there!

"Mistress Frasquita," repeated the noble Lady, seeing that the Miller's wife had not moved from her place, "I have told you that you can come in and sit down."

This second intimation was made in a voice kinder and more indulgent than the former. You would have said that her Ladyship, on observing the restrained bearing and the robust beauty of the woman before her, had in her turn instinctively divined that she had to do, here, with no low and contemptible being, but rather perhaps with another unhappy creature like herself—unhappy in the single fact of having known the Corregidor!

Then those two women, who supposed themselves doubly rivals, looked at each other with calm and indulgent eyes and discovered, to their surprise, that their souls took pleasure in one another, like two strangers who meet and know themselves for brothers.

Not otherwise do the pure snows of lofty mountains behold and hail each other from afar.

Tasting these sweet emotions, the Miller's wife advanced with dignified carriage into the salon and seated herself on the edge of a chair.

On her brief return to the Mill, foreseeing that she would

have to pay some important calls in the City, she had taken the opportunity to set herself somewhat in order and had put on a black woollen mantilla with a plush fringe, which suited her divinely. She looked every inch a Lady.

As for the Corregidor, it is said that throughout that episode he remained completely silent. The growl of Mistress Frasquita and her appearance on the scene had, of course, startled him extremely. That woman inspired in him a greater terror than his own wife.

"Now, Miller Lucas," pursued Doña Mercedes, turning to her husband; "here is Mistress Frasquita. You can now put your question again. You can ask her of this business about your honor."

"Mercedes! By Christ's nails!" cried the Corregidor. "You don't know, it seems, what I am capable of. Again I solemnly conjure you to leave joking and tell me all that has happened here during my absence. Where is this fellow?"

"Who? My husband? My husband is getting up and cannot be much longer in coming."

"Getting up!" roared Don Eugenio.

"You are surprised? Then where would you have an honest man be, at this time of night, but at home, in bed, and asleep with his lawful wife, as God commands?"

"My dear Mercedes! Watch your words! Remember that others hear us! Remember that I am the Corregidor!"

"Don't shout at *me*, Miller Lucas, or I shall send for the

Bailiffs to take you to jail!" replied her Ladyship, rising to her feet.

"Me to jail? Me? The Corregidor of the City!"

"The Corregidor of the City, the representative of the Law, the King's proxy," replied the great Lady with a sternness and energy that drowned the voice of the pretended Miller, "arrived home at the proper hour, to rest from the noble labors of his office, to continue tomorrow his task of defending the honor and lives of the citizens, the sanctity of the hearth and the modesty of women, thus providing that no one, dressed up as a Corregidor or any other thing, shall enter the bedrooms of other men's wives; that no one shall surprise virtue in its unguarded moments of repose, that no one shall abuse its innocent sleep."

"Mercedes! Of what are you speaking?" exclaimed the Corregidor, and his lips and gums whistled the words. "If such a thing has happened in my house, then, I say, you are nothing but a wicked, perfidious, and licentious creature."

"To whom is this fellow speaking?" her Ladyship broke out disdainfully, casting her eyes over those that stood about her. "Who is this madman? Who is this tipsy rascal? I cannot even believe now that it is an honest miller like Miller Lucas, although this rustic suit is his. Señor Juan López, believe what I say," she continued, turning to the Village Mayor who stood there appalled. "My husband, the Corregidor of the City, came home two hours ago, with his three-cornered hat, his scarlet cloak, his knightly sword, and his staff of authority. The servants and Bailiffs who are here listening to me, rose up and saluted when they saw him pass through the porch, up the staircase, and across the hall. After that they locked all the doors, and since then no one has got into the house until you all arrived. Is this so? Answer, all!"

"It's true! It's quite true!" answered the Wet-Nurse, the servants, and the underlings, all of whom, grouped about the door of the salon, were assisting at this singular scene.

"Out of here, everybody!" roared Don Eugenio, foaming with rage. "Weasel! Weasel! Arrest all these vile creatures who don't know how to respect me! To jail with the lot of them! To the gallows with the whole crew!"

Weasel was nowhere to be seen.

"For the rest, Sir," continued Doña Mercedes, changing her tone and deigning now to look at her husband and to treat him as such, for she began to fear that the jest might go too far, "we will suppose that you are my husband. We will suppose that you are Don Eugenio de Zúñiga y Ponce de León."

"And so I am!"

"We will suppose, too, that I am somewhat to blame for having mistaken for you a man who came into my bedroom dressed as a Corregidor..."

"Infamous rogues!" cried the old man, clapping his hand

to his side and finding himself left in the lurch with the Miller's sash in place of a sword.

The Miller's wife covered her face with one side of her mantilla to hide her jealous tears.

"Let us assume whatever you wish," continued Doña Mercedes with indescribable calm. "But tell me now, my Lord; what right have you to complain? Can you stand up as counsel for the prosecution and accuse me? Can you sentence me, as judge? Have you, by chance, just returned from the Sermon, or from Confession, or from hearing Mass? Or what is it that you are returning from in this dress and with this lady? Where have you been passing half the night?"

"Allow me…" exclaimed Mistress Frasquita, rising to her feet as if lifted by a spring and throwing herself proudly between her Ladyship and her husband.

The latter, who was about to speak, stood open-mouthed on seeing that the Miller's wife was entering the fray.

But her Ladyship anticipated her.

"I will not trouble you, Ma'am," she said, "to waste explanations on *me*. I demand none; far from it! But here comes one who has a right to demand them! Settle your affairs with *him!*"

At that moment a door that led into a closet was thrown open and there stood Miller Lucas, dressed from top to toe as a Corregidor, with staff, gloves, and sword, as if in the very act of entering the Council Chamber of the Corporation.

XXXII. FAITH MOVES MOUNTAINS

"A VERY good evening to you all!" The new arrival, doffing his three-cornered hat, pronounced his greeting with the mouthing utterance peculiar to Don Eugenio de Zúñiga. And thereupon he stepped into the salon, swaying in all directions, and went to kiss her Ladyship's hand.

The whole party was thunderstruck. Miller Lucas's resemblance to the real Corregidor was astounding. The servants, and even Señor Juan López himself, could not restrain a guffaw of laughter.

Under this new affront Don Eugenio flung himself upon Miller Lucas with the eyes of a basilisk.

But Mistress Frasquita blocked his way. She put the Corregidor aside with that arm of which he had had more than enough experience already, and his Honor, to avoid another somersault and the consequent humiliation, gave in without a murmur. Evidently the woman was born to be the master of the poor old man.

At the sight of his wife standing before him, Miller Lucas turned pale as death; but he controlled himself and, with a laugh so horrible that it forced him to clap his hand to his heart lest it should burst, he said to her, still imitating the Corregidor:

"God bless you, Frasquita! Have you sent your nephew his nomination yet?"

Then you should have seen the Miller's wife. She threw back her mantilla, raised her head with the majesty of a lioness, and fixing on the false Corregidor two eyes like two daggers, she flung her answer in his face:

"Lucas, I despise you!"

All believed that she had spat at him; such violence did her gesture, her attitude, and the tone of her voice impart to the phrase.

When he heard his wife's voice, the Miller's face was transfigured. A kind of heavenly inspiration had pierced his soul, flooding it with light and gladness: so that, forgetting for the moment all that he had seen and thought he had seen at the Mill, he cried out, with tears in his eyes and sincerity on his lips:

"Then you are my own Frasquita?"

"No!" answered the Miller's wife, beside herself with anger, "I am not your Frasquita! I am...! Ask all your fine doings of tonight, they'll tell you what you have made of the heart that loved you so!"

And she fell aweeping like an ice mountain that collapses and slowly turns to water.

Her Ladyship, who could contain herself no longer, went towards her and gathered her in her arms with great tenderness. And then Mistress Frasquita fell to kissing her, hardly knowing what she did, murmuring to her between her sobs, like a child that seeks refuge in its mother:

135

"My Lady! My Lady! How unhappy I am!"

"Not so unhappy as you think!" answered her Lady-ship, her generous heart touched to tears.

"And how unhappy am I!" groaned Miller Lucas at the same time, struggling against the tears that he was ashamed to shed.

"And what about me?" Don Eugenio broke out at last, softened by the contagious grief of the others, or hoping, himself too, to escape by the watery way: I mean, by the vale of tears. "Ah! I'm a sinful man, a monster, a worthless rogue who has only got his deserts!"

And he began to bellow mournfully as he clasped the paunch of Señor Juan López.

And the latter and all the servants wept similarly, and it seemed that all was concluded without a soul having made any explanation whatsoever.

XXXIII. WELL?

AND WHAT ABOUT YOU?

MILLER LUCAS was the first to rise above that sea of tears. The fact was, he was beginning to remember all that he had seen through the keyhole.

"Ladies and Gentlemen," he said. "Let us explain ourselves!"

"Where is the use, Miller Lucas?" exclaimed her Ladyship. "Your wife is an angel."

"Good...yes...;but..."

"I will have no buts. Let her speak; you will see how soon she proves her innocence. From the moment I first saw her, my heart told me she was a saint, in spite of all you had told me."

"Good; then let her speak!" said Miller Lucas.

"I will not speak!" answered the Miller's wife. "It's you that will have to speak, because the truth is that you..."

And Mistress Frasquita said no more, for she was silenced by her invincible respect for her Ladyship.

"Well? And what about you?" replied Miller Lucas, again losing all faith.

"It's not a question of her, now!" shouted the Corregidor, once more in the grip of his jealousy. "It's a question of you and this Lady! Ah, Mercedes! Who would have believed that you...!"

137

"Well? And what about you?" replied her Ladyship, and she measured him with her eye.

And for some moments the two couples repeated a hundred times the same phrase:

"What about you?"

"Well? and what about you?"

"Come, you!"

"No, you!"

"But how could *you* …?" Et cetera, et cetera, et cetera!

The thing would have gone on for ever had not her Ladyship, resuming her dignity, at last addressed Don Eugenio thus:

"Look you here, Sir; you keep quiet for the present. We can air our particular grievances later on. What is urgent now is to restore peace to the heart of Miller Lucas; a very simple matter, in my judgment, for I see there Señor Juan López and Tony, who are dying to prove Mistress Frasquita's innocence."

"I have no need of men to prove my innocence," replied the latter. "I have two more credible witnesses, witnesses whom no one can say that I have bribed or corrupted."

"And where are they?" asked the Miller.

"They are downstairs, at the door."

"Then tell them to come up, with her Ladyship's permission."

"The poor things couldn't come up."

"Ah, two old women, I suppose! Fine, trustworthy witnesses, and no mistake!"

"No, not women! Just two females!"

"Worse and worse! Two children, then! Perhaps you'll tell me their names."

"One is called Hazel and the other Frolic."

"Our two donkeys! Frasquita, you're making fun of me."

"No, I'm speaking quite seriously. I can prove to you, with our two donkeys as witnesses, that I was not at the Mill when you saw the Corregidor there."

"In God's name, explain!"

"Listen, Lucas! and think shame of yourself for having doubted my honor! While you were riding tonight from the Village to our house I was on my way from our house to the Village, and so we passed on the road. But you were riding off the road, or rather you had stopped to strike a light in the middle of a field…"

"Yes, it's true that I stopped! Continue!"

"At that moment your jenny brayed."

"Yes, so she did! Ah, how happy I am! Go on! Go on! Every word gives me back a year of my life!"

"And another bray on the road answered that one."

"Ah, yes! Yes! God bless you! It's as if I heard it still!"

"It was Hazel and Frolic, who had recognized each other and, like good friends, wished each other good evening, while we did neither."

"Say no more! Say no more!"

"You and I recognized each other so little that the two of us took fright and went tearing off in opposite directions. And so you see that I was not at the Mill. If you want to know now why you found the Corregidor in our bed, feel those clothes that you have on, which must still be wet, and they'll tell you better than I can. His Honor fell into the mill-race and Weasel stripped him and put him to bed. If you want to know why I opened the door, it was because I thought it was you who were drowning and shouting for me. And, lastly, if you want to know about the nomination... But I've no more to say at present. When we're alone, I'll tell you about that and other little things... which I must not mention before her Ladyship."

"All that Mistress Frasquita has said is the pure truth," cried Señor Juan López, who was anxious to curry favor with her Ladyship, seeing she was the real power at Headquarters.

"Every word of it!" added Tony, following his master's lead.

"Every word of it, so far!" added the Corregidor, much relieved that Mistress Frasquita's explanations had gone no further.

"So you're innocent!" cried Miller Lucas, submitting to the evidence. "My Frasquita! My own Frasquita! Forgive the wrong I did you and let me give you a kiss!"

"Oh, that's another sack of wheat," said the Miller's wife, recoiling from him. "Before I give you a kiss I must hear *your* explanations."

"I will give all explanations both for him and myself," said Doña Mercedes.

"I've been waiting for them for the last hour!" vouchsafed the Corregidor, trying to recover his position.

"But I shall not give them," went on her Ladyship, turning her back scornfully on her husband, "until these two gentlemen have changed back into their own clothes; and, even then, I shall give them only to the one who deserves to hear them."

"Come! Come, let us change!" said the Miller to Don Eugenio, very glad now that he had not murdered him, but still eyeing him with a truly Moorish hatred. "Your Honor's dress chokes me! I have been thoroughly miserable ever since I put it on."

"Because you don't understand how to wear it!" replied the Corregidor. "I, on the other hand, am eager to get back into it, so as to hang you and half creation with you, if my wife does not exonerate herself to my complete satisfaction."

Her Ladyship, who heard this, reassured the company with the gentle smile that belongs to those patient angels whose ministry is to watch over men.

XXXIV. HER LADYSHIP'S A FINE
WOMAN TOO!

WHEN the Corregidor and the Miller had left the salon,
her Ladyship seated herself once more on the sofa, placed
Mistress Frasquita at her side, and, turning to the servants
and underlings who crowded the doorway, said to them
with kindly simplicity:

"Now, my men: tell this excellent woman all the evil
that you know of me."

The servants came forward and ten eager voices all tried
to speak at once, but the Wet-Nurse, as the person of most
weight in the household, imposed silence on the rest, and
spoke as follows:

"You must know, Mistress Frasquita, that I and my Lady
were looking after the children tonight, waiting for the
Master to return and reciting the third Rosary to pass time
(since the message brought by Weasel had been that my
Lord the Corregidor was going out after certain very terrible criminals, and there was no question of going to bed
till we had him safe home again), when we heard the sound
of someone in the next room, which is my Lord's and my
Lady's bedroom. We snatched up the lamp, half dead with
fright, and went to see who was in the room; when, Holy
Virgin, on going in, we saw that a man dressed like my
Lord, but who was not him (since it was your husband!),

was trying to hide under the bed. 'Thieves!' we started
shouting at the top of our voices, and a minute later the
room was full of people and the Bailiffs were dragging the

sham Corregidor from his hiding-place. My Lady, who, like all of us, had recognized Miller Lucas, was afraid, seeing him in those clothes, that he had killed the Master, and began to make lamentations fit to melt a stone; while the rest of us shouted: 'To jail! To jail with him!' 'Thief! Murderer!' was the best thing that Miller Lucas heard of himself; and the truth is, he stood there like a corpse, up against the wall, not fit to say Bo to a goose. But, when he saw they were going to take him to jail, he said…what I'm just going to repeat, though in truth it would be better left unspoken: 'My Lady,' he said, 'I am neither a thief nor a murderer; the thief and the murderer…of my honor is in my house, in bed with my wife.'"

"Poor Lucas!" sighed Mistress Frasquita.

"Poor me!" murmured her Ladyship quietly.

"So we all said: 'Poor Brother Lucas and our poor Lady!' Because, to tell the truth, Mistress Frasquita, we had a notion that my Lord had fixed his eye on you; and, although nobody imagined that you…"

"Nurse!" exclaimed her Ladyship severely. "No more of that!"

"I'll go on!" said a Bailiff, seizing the opportunity to put his word in. "Miller Lucas (who fooled us properly with his clothes and his way of walking when he came in, so that we all took him for my Lord the Corregidor) had not come with the best of intentions, as you might say, and if her

Ladyship had been in bed, you can imagine what would have happened..."

"Here! That'll do for you as well!" interrupted the Cook. "You're talking nothing but nonsense. Well, yes, Mistress Frasquita: Miller Lucas, so as to explain why he was in my Mistress's bedroom, had to confess why he had come...! Well, of course, my Lady couldn't contain herself when she heard that, and she caught him a smack on the mouth that pushed half the words down his throat. I myself, I'm bound to say, called him a lot of bad names and was ready to scratch his eyes out... Because you know, Mistress Frasquita, although he's your husband, to come poaching like that on other people's preserves..."

"You're nothing but a chatterbox!" shouted the Porter, getting in front of the oratress. "What else would you have had?... Finally, Mistress Frasquita, listen to me, and we'll get to the point... Her Ladyship did and said what was worthy of her. Then, when she had got over her annoyance, she felt sorry for Miller Lucas and began to turn her mind to the bad behavior of my Lord the Corregidor, after which she spoke these words, or something like them: 'Infamous though your thought has been, Miller Lucas, and although I can never pardon such insolence, it is necessary that your wife and my husband should believe for some hours that they have been caught in their own trap, and that you, helped by this disguise, have paid them tit for tat.

The best revenge we can take on them is to play them this trick, which we can easily explain away when it suits us.' Having hit on this happy thought, her Ladyship and Miller Lucas lessoned us all in what we had to do and say when his Honor came home; and, to be sure, I caught Sebastian Weasel such a whack on the backside, that I don't think he'll forget Saint Simon and Judas's day for a bit."

When the Porter stopped talking, her Ladyship and Mistress Frasquita had been whispering together for some time, hugging and kissing each other every moment, and sometimes unable to contain their laughter.

It's a pity that what they said could not be heard! But the reader can imagine it for himself without great trouble; and, if not the reader, the readeress.

XXXV. IMPERIAL DECREE

UPON THAT, the Corregidor and Miller Lucas came back into the salon, each in his own clothes.

"Now it's my turn!" said the illustrious Don Eugenio de Zúñiga as he entered.

And, after giving two blows on the floor with his staff as if to recover his energy (like an official Antæus, who did not feel strong until his Malacca cane had touched Earth), he said to her Ladyship, with an emphasis and a coolness that cannot be described:

"Mercedes! I am waiting for your explanations!"

Meanwhile the Miller's wife had risen to her feet and had given Miller Lucas a pinch of peace that made him skip to the ceiling, while she gazed at him with reconciled and bewitching eyes.

The Corregidor, who observed this pantomime, was dumbfounded at the spectacle of so unaccountable a reconciliation.

Then he addressed himself again to his wife.

"Madam!" he said to her, as sour as vinegar, "all have reached an understanding except us! Put me out of my doubts! I order you both as husband and as Corregidor!"

And again he beat his staff on the floor.

"So you are going?" exclaimed Doña Mercedes, going over to Mistress Frasquita and paying not the slightest attention to Don Eugenio. "Then go with your mind at rest, for this scandal shall have no consequences. Rosa! Light this lady and gentleman, who tell me that they are going. Goodbye, Miller Lucas!"

"Oh, no!" shouted Don Eugenio, throwing himself in the way. "Miller Lucas cannot go! Miller Lucas is under arrest until I know the whole truth. Ho, Bailiffs! In the King's name!"

Not a single officer obeyed Don Eugenio. All fixed their eyes on her Ladyship.

"Come, Sir! Move out of the way!" she added, passing almost over her husband and bidding everyone goodbye with the greatest courtesy; that is to say, with her head on one side, holding her skirt with the tips of her fingers, bending gracefully to execute the bow which was the fashion at that time, and which was called the *pompa*.

"But I...But you...But we...But they..." the wretched old man went on mumbling, taking his wife by the dress and disturbing her in the process of her social duties.

But in vain! Nobody paid the least attention to his Honor.

When all had gone, and only the discordant couple were left in the salon, her Ladyship at last deigned to speak to her husband with such an accent as the Czarina of all the Russias might have used to fulminate upon a fallen Minister the order of perpetual exile to Siberia:

"If you live to be a thousand, you shall never know

what happened tonight in my bedroom. If you had been there, as you ought to have been, you would not be under the necessity of asking. For my part, there is not now, and there never will be, any reason for me to satisfy you; since I despise you so much that, if you were not the father of my children, I would throw you this very moment from that balcony, as I banish you for ever from my bedroom. And so, good-night, my Lord!"

Having pronounced those words, which Don Eugenio heard without so much as winking (since his courage left him when he was face to face with his wife), her Ladyship entered the closet and from there passed to her bedroom, locking the doors behind her; and the poor man was left high and dry in the middle of the salon, murmuring between his gums (not between his teeth) with a surely unparalleled cynicism:

"Well, Sir, I did not expect to get off so easily! Weasel must find me accommodation!"

XXXVI. CONCLUSION, MORAL, &
EPILOGUE

THE LITTLE BIRDS were chirping their greetings to the dawn when Miller Lucas and Mistress Frasquita left the City and turned in the direction of their Mill.

The couple travelled on foot; in front of them, side by side, walked the two donkeys.

"On Sunday you'll have to go to Confession," said the Miller's wife to her husband, "to wash yourself clean of all your evil thoughts and wicked designs of last night."

"You're quite right!" replied the Miller. "But, meanwhile, you must do me another favor, and that is to give away our bedclothes and mattress to the poor and renew the whole lot. I don't sleep where that poisonous old beast has been sweating!"

"Don't speak of him, Lucas!" answered Mistress Frasquita. "Let's talk of something else. I want another favor from you."

"You've only got to ask."

"This summer you must take me to the baths at Solán de Cabras."

"But why?"

"To see if we can't have children."

"A very good idea! I'll take you, if God gives us life."

And thereupon they reached the Mill, at the moment

when the sun, though it had not yet risen, was gilding the summits of the mountains.

*   *   *   *

In the afternoon, to the great surprise of the Miller and his wife, who expected no more visits from high personages after a scandal like that of the preceding night, there came to the Mill more gentry than ever. The venerable Bishop, several Canons, the Counsellor, two Priors, and sundry other persons (who, as afterwards appeared, had been summoned thither by the noble Prelate) quite filled the little court under the vine-arbor.

The Corregidor alone was missing.

As soon as the party was complete, the Lord Bishop spoke to the following effect: that, whereas certain events had happened in that house, his Canons and himself would continue to come there as before, so that neither the honest Miller and his wife nor the other persons there present should have any share in the public censure, incurred only by him who had profaned with his foul conduct so temperate and virtuous a gathering. He exhorted Mistress Frasquita paternally to be, for the future, less provocative and enticing in her speech and manners and to cover her arms somewhat more and wear a higher neck to her bodice. He recommended Miller Lucas to be more circumspect, less self-seeking, and less free in his intercourse with his supe-

riors, and ended by giving his blessing to all and announc-
ing that, as he was not fasting that day, he would eat with
much pleasure a couple of bunches of grapes.

All were of the same opinion, at least as regards this last
particular, and that afternoon the arbor was shaken indeed.

The Miller reckoned the consumption of grapes at no less than four stones' weight.

*   *   *   *

Those delightful gatherings continued for about three years, until contrary to everybody's expectations, the armies of Napoleon entered Spain and the War of Independence began.

The Lord Bishop, the Prebendary, and the Penitentiary died in the year 8, and the Counsellor and the other cronies in the years 9, 10, 11, and 12, unable to endure the sight of the Frenchmen, Poles, and other vermin that invaded the land and smoked their pipes in the very sanctuaries of the churches during Mass.

The Corregidor, who never again went back to the Mill, was deprived of his office by a French Marshal and died in the State Prison, because (be it said to his honor) he would not for a moment truckle to the foreign domination.

Doña Mercedes did not marry again. She brought up her children admirably, and retired in old age to a convent where she ended her days in the odor of sanctity.

Weasel went over to the French.

Señor Juan López became a Guerrilla, commanded a band, and died, as did his Bailiff, in the famous battle of Baza, after killing a great number of Frenchmen.

Lastly, Miller Lucas and Mistress Frasquita (although

they never succeeded in having children, in spite of vows and prayers and the visit to Solán de Cabras), went on loving each other in their own way and lived to a great age. They saw the end of Absolutism in 1812 and 1820, and its return in 1814 and 1823, and, at last, the establishment of the Constitutional System in good earnest at the death of the Absolute King; and they passed to a better life just at the outbreak of the Seven Years' Civil War. But the tall hats which by this time everyone was wearing never made them forget the good old times symbolized by

THE THREE-CORNERED

HAT.